A RING OF JUSTICE

TED LEIGHTON

Cover: Rebekah Wetmore
Editor: Andrew Wetmore

ISBN: 978-1-990187-44-5
First edition October, 2022

MOOSE HOUSE
PUBLICATIONS

2475 Perotte Road
Annapolis County, NS
B0S 1A0

moosehousepress.com
info@moosehousepress.com

We live and work in Mi'kma'ki, the ancestral and unceded territory of the Mi'kmaw People. This territory is covered by the "Treaties of Peace and Friendship" which Mi'kmaw and Wolastoqiyik (Maliseet) People first signed with the British Crown in 1725. The treaties did not deal with surrender of lands and resources but in fact recognized Mi'kmaq and Wolastoqiyik (Maliseet) title and established the rules for what was to be an ongoing relationship between nations. We are all Treaty people.

For Aoife McCauley,
who encouraged it all into words

Contents

Ted Leighton

From the Annapolis Royal *Spectator*

September 13, 1999

The Minister of Health was in Bridgetown today to announce a major addition to the Bridgetown Hospital. Renovations and construction of a new wing that will house an expanded emergency room will begin this week.

The entire project is a gift to the hospital by Ontario businessman George Ferrante in recognition of the expert emergency service that saved the life of his son this past summer.

William Ferrante and a friend were on a motorcycle tour of Nova Scotia in July when they gathered, cooked and ate a meal of mussels at nearby Hampton. Shortly afterwards, they felt tingling in their hands and feet, became dizzy and nauseated, and experienced some difficulty breathing. They sought help at a nearby house and were driven immediately to the Bridgetown Hospital.

Dr. Jane Harvey examined them, and then asked what the young men had eaten that day. On hearing of the large meal of mussels, together with the patients' symptoms, she suspected paralytic shellfish poisoning. She sedated the two young men, inserted breathing tubes into their windpipes to permit mechanically assisted breathing and sent them by ambulance to the intensive care unit in Halifax. They were maintained there on full life support for two days until quite suddenly their muscle paralysis ended, and they recovered completely within a few hours.

The Medical Director said that the insightful diagnosis of paralytic shellfish poisoning, immediate intubation for mechanical breathing and emergency transport to Halifax had avoided what otherwise would have been certain death for the two young men.

William Ferrante told The Spectator *that paralytic shellfish poisoning was a terrifying experience. He was completely paralyzed and unable to breathe or even move his eyes, yet his mind and all his senses were fully active; touch, pain, vision, hearing, smell, taste all were unaffected by the poisoning. During the last day, medical staff discussed whether life support should be discontinued because the two young men seemed so nearly dead. He had no way to let them know that he was still alive or to beg them not to disconnect him.*

It was the terror that Billy Ferrante most remembered, a terror like being buried alive. More than anything, he craved the power to create that same terror in others.

Ted Leighton

1: Stinks!

"Fred, please leave your semen on the back steps."

It seemed an odd note, Rick Robichaud thought, after he had regained his balance and could look down to read it. The note was held in place by the edge of a big shipping container filled with liquid nitrogen. It was in Zora's handwriting and was the sort of note he had learned that veterinarians sometimes write. *How many households have a regular semen delivery man?*

He marvelled to himself that half the genes for the next generation of calves in the whole district were in suspended animation inside that container.

Rick had stepped out the door with Bronwyn in one hand and a basket of wet laundry in the other, and he was pleased at the dexterity with which he had avoided falling after tripping over the unexpected obstacle. He put Bronwyn in the basket and tickled her each time he stooped to take out another wet item and attach it to the clothesline. He knew this trick wouldn't work much longer; Bronwyn was getting bigger and stronger every day.

Right: diaper change, nap time, bread and casserole out of the oven, load the courier truck with

cheese. Rick moved the frozen semen inside the house and down to Zora's clinic at the back.

He had Bronwyn napping in 15 minutes through good luck and the magic of Erik Satie's nocturnes. He fired up the baby monitor app on his phone to watch Bronwyn as she slept, got the rest of the day's food organized and was at the dairy behind the house, 'la fromagerie' as his uncle Gilles had insisted on calling it, in 15 minutes more.

Lansdowne Highland Cheese was abuzz with activity; the staff were deeply into making cheddar from the evening and morning milking. The delivery truck for Halifax and Montreal was just pulling in. The shipments were ready to go, old cheddar and Stilton-style blue. Rick reviewed the paper work, signed off, and helped load the truck.

Bronwyn was still out cold, so he ran to the barn to check in with the farm hands. This was mostly Zora's domain, but the daily logistics of feed in, and manure and milk out, fell mostly to him. Highland cows are small but 150 of them still turn over a lot of material.

It all worked so smoothly, though, that Rick and Zora's attention was only required when something within their competence went wrong. The staff knew way more about how to run the farm and dairy than they did. They were the newbies.

Big noise from the monitor: Bronwyn was awake and ready to go.

Rick did the 100-yard dash to the house, and soon was in the kitchen rocking chair giving Bronwyn her mid-morning top-up from the just-warmed bottle. He was starting to get good at this job.

With Bronwyn supported along his left arm, guzzling lustily, he could steady her bottle with his left hand and reach the cup of hot coffee on the side table with his right, hot because he had learned to have a cup ready to go beside the microwave to heat when he warmed the milk, for him to nurse when he nursed Bronwyn.

"Oh, Zori, where are you now?" he sighed, managing the day's first little wave of lonely exhaustion.

He knew perfectly well where she was. Dr Zora Cromwell was back doing her veterinary rounds again after six months of maternity leave—saving animals, driving and pumping her own milk between calls, helping farmers make a living. His beautiful wonderful partner for life, doing again what she had always most wanted to do.

He looked down at Bronwyn, who was eagerly draining her bottle of mother-in-absentia. He couldn't really feel that special physical and emotional sensation between a nursing mother and her child. Nonetheless, he felt a special bond with Bronwyn around the fact that they both had a profound emotional and physical attachment to the two exquisite sources of all that milk, and he figured his attachment would outlast hers by quite a few decades.

Time to be off to Marie's, and fast. Zora would be home at noon, baby-starved and expecting a good lunch for herself, too, and to be out the door again at 1:00.

Rick wanted Marie to pass judgment on the new cheese Lansdowne Highland had invented while trying to salvage a batch of Stilton from a big mistake made by a visiting WWOOFer. It had sold out like it was pure gold from the little sales counter in la fromagerie. Before they made it a production item, he wanted a professional gourmet's critical opinion.

Bronwyn had recently taken offence to all vehicle travel, expressed mostly by nonstop high-decibel screaming. Rick braced himself and launched into action: diaper change, outdoor clothes, reload the everything-you-need-for-the-baby bag, shoes, some different car toys, the almost forgotten box of cheese, and everything out and into the truck. Bronwyn began screaming the moment she hit the car seat, the scream rising in tone and intensity as Rick strapped her in, got in himself and drove off.

It was only a 15-minute drive to Morganville on the dusty back road, not quite long enough, Rick hoped, for Bronwyn to exhaust herself, fall asleep, and screw up the rest of the day's schedule. Bronwyn was in high form today, however, and by the time they arrived she had advanced into a full raging tantrum.

As he came up the driveway, Rick saw Jeremy, the young man who lived across the road, on Marie's back deck. Eureka! Jeremy to the rescue, maybe. You could never be sure with Jeremy.

Rick leaped out of the truck, loosened and removed the screaming Bronwyn, greeted Jeremy with a brief word and held out to him the howling baby.

Jeremy showed no surprise or other emotion. He took the screaming child awkwardly and held her at an odd angle against his chest with both arms. Bronwyn stopped mid-scream, wriggled a little, and began to coo.

"Do you want to hold her, Jerry?" Rick asked, trying not to sound too eager. Jeremy gave a poker-faced affirmative nod. "Is Marie home?" Rick stepped lightly toward the door.

"Shop," Jeremy answered.

Rick redirected his momentarily carefree steps toward the big building a little away from the house, where Marie did her mechanic work. She was just banging a new ball joint into Lisa Willson's old beater with a small sledgehammer when Rick walked in. Dressed for this kind of work, she looked to Rick like a late-career Hollywood beauty miscast as a factory worker.

She nodded to Rick, gave the joint a final bang, bolted on the brace, gave the whole thing a hard pry with a crowbar to see if everything was properly in place, then hit the switch to lower the car to the ground. "That'll still be in good shape when the rest of the car has fallen apart," she said as she released her stylish red hair from under her greasy hat, stepped out of her baggy coveralls and exchanged boots for sandals. "Where's that cheese?"

They found Jeremy still on the deck, with Bronwyn peeking bright-eyed at the world over his shoulder. Her face brightened when she saw Rick, but she gave no sign of wanting him to take her from

Jeremy.

"Melvin Prime is coming at noon to pick up Jerry to go to his camp for a few days," Marie said. "Let's go in. I want Jerry to have a good lunch before he goes. Bring in that cheese and we'll try it."

In the kitchen, Marie quickly put three pieces of bread in the toaster, placed jars of peanut butter and jam out on the counter and partially filled a pint-sized glass with orange juice. For herself, she filled a wine glass about ¼ full from an expensive-looking bottle of Malbec, put a few cream crackers on a cutting board and slowly transferred a slightly-resisting Bronwyn from Jeremy to herself.

"Jerry, get your lunch together while I try this cheese. Just carve it up on that board, Ricky. How's my Bronnie today?"

As Marie fussed and giggled with Bronwyn, the men got to work. Jeremy methodically made a tall sandwich of the three pieces of toast, interleaving two thick layers of peanut butter and jam. He then rolled the whole thing into a tight cylinder and forced it slowly into the glass of orange juice, which rose up around it and was absorbed into the toast. He began eating it with a spoon.

Rick took out the cheese, a white round the size and shape of a double-thick Camembert. He cut it in two, revealing a creamy, heavily blue-streaked interior that resembled melting blueberry-ripple ice cream and emitted a powerful aroma that left no doubt that this was serious cheese.

Jeremy gagged on the smell and moved to the

other side of the room. "Stinks!" he said.

Rick smoothed a creamy layer onto a cracker and handed it to Marie, making another one for himself. Rick did not know much about cheeses, but he had a hunch that this one might be a winner, even though Lansdowne Highland had never intended to invent it.

He watched Marie closely as she sniffed, then licked, then took a bite of the stuff. Her expression was totally non-committal. She waved a cheesy bit of cracker in front of Bronwyn's nose and Bronwyn defecated explosively into her diaper.

Marie took another bite of cheese and a sip of wine and went face-neutral again. She handed Bronwyn back to Rick, put a big mess of cheese on a half cracker and took it in one big bite, chasing it again with wine.

"Is this the second batch?"

"Third"

"All the same?"

"Yup."

"It's a million-dollar cheese, Ricky, if you want a million dollars, but I'm sure you don't. How much of this stuff do you want to make?"

Rick thought for a moment as he shifted around the struggling Bronwyn. "Not so much. Maybe a thousand per year, to use the milk we use in tourist season for feta. Otherwise, we'd have to expand everything, and we already are as big as we want to be."

"Right," Marie said. "Let me send a few to a cheese

stall in the Old Montreal Market. You can wholesale this stuff for a good $40 a pound in the exclusive restaurant trade. That's this stall's business. They'll take all of it if they take any. You can drop the price around here to something affordable and still make plenty of money. You'll need a catchy name for it."

The sound of tires on driveway signalled that Mel had arrived and, if he was on time, that Rick and Bronwyn were going to be seriously late getting home to Zora. Rick imagined another 15 minutes of Bronwyn screaming all the way home as he quickly changed her diaper on the kitchen counter.

Then he had an inspiration. "Jerry, could you put Bronnie in her car seat and buckle her in?" Jeremy looked doubtful.

"Don't know how," he said.

"Just bring her out and I'll help you," Rick urged, and out they went.

Bronwyn began the usual complaints as she found herself inserted into the car seat, but as Jeremy leaned over her, fumbling with the straps and attachments, she seemed to lose her usual piss and vinegar.

She looked up at him serenely, watched him through the window as the truck backed down the driveway and kept up a quiet self-satisfied banter to herself all the way home.

2: Injustice

William Ferrante knew how to look reliable. Today it would be in a light three-piece suit, a white shirt and a muted tie, with well-polished shoes, a fresh shave and haircut. This would not have worked so well among his old motorcycle gangmates, or among his drinking buddies and girlfriends, but it was just right for Thomas French, QC.

In his office high above Bloor Street, the lawyer welcomed William cordially but not warmly, a distinction William did not recognize in any case. "I'm so sorry that your stepmother Rose was taken from us so unexpectedly," the lawyer began. "I'm devastated really—a drunk driver speeding down the road and suddenly she's gone. My wife and I had the greatest respect for her and always enjoyed her company."

Thomas French had been the main legal counsel for the family for almost 40 years. William was not his favourite client, but he owed it to his old friend George, William's father, and to the whole family, to do his best for all of them.

"I'm the only one left now," William said with an exaggerated sigh. "That's why I made this appoint-

19

ment to see you. I didn't see my stepmother often over the past several years and so I don't know in what forms the various family trusts and accounts have been left to me. I want to take proper responsibility for them now. I understand you are the executor of Rose's will, so I have come to you in that capacity for information, and also, as a family friend, for guidance."

Thomas French steeled himself for what was sure to follow. "Rose's death has not changed anything with respect to your personal finances, William," he said. "As you know, she was highly placed in the finance world herself and she made no use of the trust funds your father left to her sixteen years ago. That trust money now has gone to the nature conservation societies stipulated in your father's and her wills. She left her own wealth to several charities associated with mental health research. She also left a contribution to the trust still being held in your brother's name, of which she was the principal trustee after your father died."

Emotion flashed briefly in William's eyes as the lawyer made this last point. He looked down and then at Thomas French again. "My father left Julian way more than he left me. Julian's own will left all of his wealth to me when he died 15 years ago. Why hasn't Julian's will been honoured and properly executed?"

"Well, as you know, your father thought Julian would need a lifetime of care due to his sometimes-difficult mental condition, whatever it actually was.

He left him enough to ensure he could receive the assistance he would need as long as he might live. You are almost a decade older than Julian and your father thought you were well set up to make your own way in the world. Both you and Julian inherited a great deal of money; your father was a very wealthy man."

"But when Julian died, all that family wealth should have come to me," William said with growing emphasis. "He had been living with me for a whole year by then. I was taking care of him day and night. Rose took all of Julian's money for herself."

"Rose did not need that money, William, but she was greatly troubled by Julian's death. She was very fond of Julian and was very much his mother for most of his life. You'll remember that his body disappeared just before it was to be cremated and it was never found. Rose could not shake off the sentimental feeling that Julian might somehow still be alive. His will had no legal status because he was only 14 years old when he signed it. But Rose refused to let Julian's inheritance be dispersed to charities, as stipulated in the articles of the trust. She felt that all such legal proceedings were premature in the same way she felt that Julian's death itself had been premature."

"But now Rose herself is dead. She can't block these proper legal processes anymore. Julian's will should take precedence now. That inheritance belongs to me."

William's anger had been rising throughout this

conversation and Thomas French could feel it was about to boil over, as it always did. To explain Rose's will any further was going to require him to find a path through a tricky labyrinth of client confidentialities.

"In 2014," he said, "Rose moved all funds held in Julian's name into a new trust. The new trust stipulates that the funds are to be held and accumulate interest until either Julian himself turns up, alive after all, and claims his inheritance, in which case he becomes the sole beneficiary of the trust, or until the year 2089, when Julian would have been 100 years old. If the funds are unclaimed by 2089, they will be disbursed to a list of charities Rose provided, or to equivalent charities of that future time."

William leapt to his feet. "That money is mine!" he shouted. "You and Rose and everyone else are trying to keep me from having it, but you can't. I've got friends too, with law degrees and without, and they will make your life so miserable you'll beg me to take what's mine. You and all the other bastards are squeezing blood out of my inheritance for your own fat salaries, more and more every month, until it'll all be gone. You won't get away with it. They won't get away with it. You'll see what'll happen. I'm only just starting on this."

As William's voice grew hysterical, two burly men appeared at the office door, and now one of them spoke. "Mr. Ferrante, I think it is time for you to go now."

William whirled around, picking up his heavy

wooden chair as he did so, and smashed the chair into the two men. He leaned across Tom French's wide desk and punched him in the face as hard as he was able on such a long reach. He ran out into the hall, kicked a deep dent in a closed elevator door, and disappeared down the stairwell.

Thomas French wiped the blood off his face with the moist towel his frightened office staff had brought to him. He apologized to the burly men he had recruited from the mail room. He asked the staff not to call any authorities, saying that he was sure they would never see Ferrante in their office again.

And he reflected on what he had managed to keep from William Ferrante: that his stepmother Rose had believed that William had killed both his father and his brother Julian, and that Julian already had returned from the dead to claim his inheritance.

3: What did those trees say?

Mel attached a regulation paper target to a board with thumbtacks, got out an old ladder and nailed the board eight feet off the ground to a big tree trunk on the far side of the cabin clearing. He put 20 shells in his old .22, pumped one into the chamber, rested his left arm on the corner of the cabin for stability, took careful aim, and fired—*bang*.

A small spot appeared on the paper target an inch or two outside the largest circle.

He pumped in a new shell and tried again—*bang*.

This time a spot appeared at the edge of the outermost circle.

"That tree is 100 feet away, so you don't often hit the bullseye," he said.

Mel hadn't known quite what he and Jeremy were going to do during their week together at his cabin on Crouse Lake, but he thought a bit of shooting practice might be a novelty and worth a try. For some reason, he had really come to like Jeremy, odd as he was. Jeremy seemed to like him too in his own unspoken way, so Mel was sure things would work out somehow.

"Ever shoot a gun before?" Mel asked.

Jeremy offered his usual poker face by way of an answer.

"Want to try?"

Jeremy gave a single forward nod.

"Safety first," Mel said. "Remember, the bullet that comes out of this thing can kill a person. Don't point it at anything you don't intend to shoot." He handed the rifle to Jeremy.

Jeremy studied the rifle as if it were an alien object. Then he put it to his shoulder as Mel had done, looked along the barrel at the target and pulled the trigger—*bang*.

The board shifted but Mel couldn't make out where it had been hit. "Was that a hit or a miss?" he asked Jeremy, who still had youthful eyes.

"Bullseye," Jeremy said without emotion.

"You son of a bitch," Mel said, not quite believing him. "You do that a second time."

Bang—dead centre again. *Bang, bang, bang, bang* —all dead centre, Jeremy just standing there, not leaning on anything.

Jeremy gave the gun a very fast, hard pump and the ejected shell flew high up in the air—*bang.* He shot the shell out of the air before it hit the ground.

Jeremy let out what sounded like a celebratory chuckle. He did a little dance as he chortled and wailed, turning himself once around in place.

Then he went poker-faced again and handed the rifle to Mel while looking half away. "Loaded," he said, which was true; they had not shot all 20 shells.

Jeremy turned away, walked down to the lake,

took off all his clothes, and jumped in the water.

Mel had supper on the table by the time Jeremy came up from the lake: liver and onions, potatoes and bread, a big bottle of ketchup, and canned fruit —just right for the first night at camp. They both ate like trenchermen.

Conversation was not something Jeremy did, but Mel still had to try; there was just too much at stake. He was sure that no one in Digby County had shot a gun like Jeremy had just done since the days of Digby's legendary Sheriff Henry Smith, whom his grandfather used to talk about and had seen as a boy. *Where did it come from?*

"You musta' shot a gun before," he ventured.

Jeremy looked down at his plate but then nodded once.

"Where'd you learn it so good?"

Jeremy said nothing, mashing bits of liver, potato and ketchup together on his plate with determination. "Don't know," he said after a few minutes, surprising Mel with such a direct answer.

"One of those things that just kind of slipped your mind I guess, eh?" Mel offered.

No response.

They were into the fruit cocktail now, with a few pantry cookies to balance out all the juice. Mel made sure that the one cherry in the can went into Jeremy's bowl.

When Mel put the bowl in front of him, Jeremy stared at the bright red cherry for a while, then picked it out of his bowl with a spoon and, almost lovingly, placed it in Mel's. Then he looked Mel straight in the eye, another first for Mel, and held his stare until Mel, finally realizing what he was waiting for, took the cherry with his own spoon and ate it.

The next day, they went by canoe and carry to Lake Franklin to catch a supper of trout in the dead-water.

"Jeremy Franklin, hey, this must be your lake," Mel joked.

He needed a joke. Jeremy was the most useless paddler Mel had ever been with in a canoe. Just hopeless! No stroke, no power, no rhythm, no nothing. He'd sit in the bow seat without moving for minutes at a time, then flail the paddle around to no apparent purpose. Once he just threw it overboard and reacted not at all to Mel's curses and labour to turn around and retrieve it.

At the carry, Jeremy leapt out of the canoe and disappeared up the trail without a word, leaving Mel to lug the canoe and paddles and fishing poles and two back packs the half mile to the dead-water, all by himself.

On the way back, Mel used the pretext of a lesson in canoe carrying to load Jeremy up with all those same articles and have him carry them down the trail. Mel followed with his fishing pole, their six trout and a stream of verbal encouragement.

On the other hand, no matter where they went or how they got there, Jeremy always seemed to know exactly where he was and where everything else was. *Youthful eyes*, Mel figured; they could see all the details his older eyes now missed.

But there was more to it than just seeing.

"Where does that carry begin?" Mel complained, as he scanned the shoreline ahead of the canoe.

"There," Jeremy had said, pointing right at the correct spot half a mile away.

"Where's my cabin from here?" Mel asked during lunch.

Jeremy stuck out one arm like a compass needle and turned to point exactly in the straight-line direction to Mel's camp.

Mel probed further. "Where'd we leave my truck?"

Jeremy corrected his compass needle arm to the west by about 20 degrees, which would have been about right.

"Where's your house? Where's my house?"

Mel himself would have needed a map and compass to know if Jeremy's responses were correct; but he responded immediately, without any time for thought or calculation, and the directions he pointed in seemed highly plausible.

Each day they did a little target practice with the .22 since Jeremy enjoyed it so much. Mel gave up all pretense of being the crack shot he once thought he was and turned his mind to invention. He put jar lids on trees at various distances as targets until Jeremy had shot them all away, then tried targets swinging at the end of a rope. Mel then tried throwing things up in the air. He started with tin cans filled with enough soil to be easy to throw up high and big enough to hit, perhaps. They soon ran out of cans; it seemed Jeremy just could never miss.

The last thing Mel threw up was a hard-boiled egg he figured was too stale to eat.

Bang.

One evening, Mel pulled the bunk bed away from its corner of the room and retrieved a larger rifle from behind a board. "Here's another one," he said. "This used to be my deer rifle, a .30-30, my pride and joy. I don't go hunting any more."

Mel worked the bolt, removed it, and looked down the barrel at the lamp—still shiny clean, ten years or more since he had fired it last. He reinserted the bolt and handed the rifle to Jeremy. "This takes big shells like those empties on the windowsill," he said. "I thought we could try shooting it, but I left my box of shells in the truck."

Jeremy looked at the rifle briefly and then set it on the table. He got up and studied the empty shells for a moment, then lay down on his bed and went to sleep.

Mel poured himself three fat fingers of rye in a wide-bottomed glass, added a little maple syrup and water, and sipped away at it thoughtfully in the soft light of the single oil lamp until he, too, was ready for sleep.

Mel woke at dawn, as usual. Jeremy was still fast asleep. It was a cold morning and as Mel fired up the wood-burning cook stove and went about making coffee and breakfast, he was surprised to discover his box of .30-30 shells in the middle of the table. *How the hell did those get there?*

His loud expletives must have roused Jeremy, who hopped out of bed.

"How the sweet lovin' Jeeeses did these get here?" he bellowed, pointing at the box of shells.

"Truck," Jeremy said. He took Mel's keys out of his own pants pocket and returned them to their habitual place in Mel's jacket.

"How?"

"Walked."

"At night?"

"Nice; trees talking."

And what did those trees say to you? Mel wondered to himself. What did Jeremy hear in the dark night forest that no one else maybe could even imagine? There was more to this young man than just a list of oddities. What word did the kids always use these days? "Awesome?" That seemed like the right word for Jeremy.

They had arrived at the camp by canoe. In a straight line, it was a mile each way to the truck through the woods, with no path, no road, no moon, in the pitch dark. Mel wouldn't have gotten a hundred feet before losing his way and falling down. He hadn't heard Jeremy leave and hadn't heard him come back in, but here he was, not one bit lost, well-slept, eyeing the pan full of bacon and the pancake batter like a hungry bear, and here were the shells. So?

Just so what the hell, that's all! Mel thought, and he flipped a big pancake high up into the air.

It was their last day at the cabin and as Mel began

cleaning up after breakfast, he found that one of the mouse traps in his trapline inside the cabin had a victim, bug-eyed, cold, stiff and stone dead. He extracted it, reset the trap and went to toss the carcass into the wood stove fire.

"No!" Jeremy screamed from across the room.

Mel stopped in mid-swing and looked at Jeremy, dumbfounded.

Jeremy ran to Mel, grabbed the mouse and quickly stepped outside. Mel heard a few dull thuds.

Then Jeremy returned and held out the mouse to him by its tail, this time with its head crushed beyond recognition. "Maybe wasn't dead," he said.

Mel took the mouse and Jeremy watched in anxious horror as Mel threw it into the flames. Jeremy held the fire box door open and watched, shivering, as the mouse gradually burned to cinders.

Mel watched Jeremy, trying to comprehend what was happening. Something really big was going on inside this enigmatic young man's heart, but Mel could not understand what it was.

Mel said it would be safe enough if they shot the .30-30 across the lake toward the outflow, especially on a Thursday morning when no one would ever come out this way.

It was an old single-shot model, and Mel decided to give Jeremy a little lecture on high-powered gun physics before letting him shoot it. The bullet would cross the line of sight twice; at about 100 feet and again at about 200 feet. At these two distances, you would hit what you aimed at. In between, you had to aim a bit low and, further out, you had to aim a bit high. Best not to try to shoot something that far away anyway.

"The kick of the discharge might hurt you if you don't hold the stock pressed tight against your shoulder" he said. "These bullets are old, heavy, lead hollow-points. Nobody uses them now for hunting because they make such a huge, messy hole in whatever they hit."

Mel put a shell in the chamber and looked down range. "Let's see if I can hit that old dead tree on the far shore," he said.

Bam! The water exploded about 20 feet in front of the tree.

"Too far away, didn't aim high enough," he concluded.

He handed the rifle to Jeremy. "Here, you try. You're the sharp-shooter. Aim for that band of white birch bark you can see on the big branch of that dead tree I was trying for."

Mel handed Jeremy a new shell and took up a position behind him so he could watch him aim and fire.

At first, Jeremy seemed to aim right at the white spot. But then he let the barrel drift up and off to the left.

"Get your aim back, Jerry—"

Bam!

The branch of the snag splintered and fell away at the spot where the birch bark had been.

"Wind." Jeremy said.

"Shit!" Mel said. It was like the kid was taking his

final exam at sniper school, and with open sights!

A moderate wind had sprung up from the northwest. It was going to make their paddle back to the truck longer and harder, especially with Mel having to do all the paddling, but Mel didn't give a damn.

He scoured out the gun barrel with brush and solvent and oil until it was shiny clean again, and put the .30-30 back in its hiding place in the corner.

4: Smoothness, strength, hardness

"We've been in the woods for a week," Mel said. "Let's go get lunch in town." Neither he nor Jeremy were ones to worry much about showers and clean clothes; a week in the woods provided a cleansing of a deeper kind.

Jeremy didn't say no, so past his place they went and down the river road, following the West Branch all the way to tidewater. Why an old meat and potatoes guy from the last century like him had fallen for hummus and feta on focaccia was a puzzle to Mel; but fallen he had, head over heels, and the best in the county was right here.

The place was busy; it was full-on tourist season. They found a table in a corner by the windows so Jeremy could have his back to a wall and see whatever was going on inside and out.

There were three main items on the short menu plus a squash soup, so they ordered two soups, two hummus extravaganzas, one each of the other two sandwiches, and non-stop coffee. Not that they hadn't eaten well at camp, but they were in a mood to celebrate the magnificence of their week together, or at least Mel was. He hoped Jeremy was too, in his own way.

There always was art on the walls of this café. It seemed to change every few months. Mel knew nothing about art, but the bright colours and changing displays always made him feel happy and welcome.

The café door flew open and Lisa Willson swept in. She ran up and kissed the barista, who happened to be her husband, then got a coffee to go. When she saw Jeremy, she came right over to their table, giving him a gentle squeeze on one shoulder and Mel a little hug.

"You guys were out in the woods for a whole week, how did it go?"

Mel gave her a quick summary. "Jerry can find his way in the woods like you wouldn't believe. I'd take him over a GPS anytime."

"He's pretty special," Lisa agreed. "Jerry, how's that wrist doing? Any more pain?"

One of Lisa's nursing jobs was to make a weekly visit to Jeremy to make sure he was looking after his health.

"Fine," Jeremy replied, looking quickly at Lisa and then away.

"Great," Lisa replied. "Gotta run now. Jerry, I'll see you on Wednesday, on my way back from Bonnie Cheever's." And off she went, just as their food started arriving.

Mel had been keeping an eye on a grim-faced,

middle-aged man sitting alone across the room, watching the busy restaurant like a fox watching chickens: Rex Cheever, Bonnie's son. Now Rex stood up and came over to their table and pulled up a chair.

"Nice little piece, that Lisa," he said to Jeremy. "You have fun with her when she visits you?"

Jeremy turned away from Rex and looked out the window.

"I guess he's too kooky anyway," Rex said, this time to Mel.

"What's up Rex?" Mel asked. "Something on your mind?"

"Just thought I'd say hello and see how the crazy guy's doin'."

"Jeremy's doing 110%. We were just getting into our meal."

"I'm surprised an old guy like you can eat this stuff. The coffee's good, but this hippy-dippy food…"

Just then, three twenty-something young ladies came in and sat down at a table for four. Rex stared fixedly at them as they settled in, removing jackets, adjusting hair. He abruptly left Mel and Jeremy, approached the girls, and talked his way into the fourth chair at their table.

Mel tried to ignore Rex and enjoy his meal, but he couldn't. He watched as the initial talk between Rex and the girls changed to few words and strained looks. Quite soon, the girls rose together, ordered takeout coffee from the cashier, and left.

Rex sat by himself for a while at their table, and

then stalked out.

Jeremy seemed to have ignored Rex and was well tucked into his second course, so Mel decided to follow his good example. It was the meal he had wanted, and he quickly got fully engaged with it.

As the lunch hour frenzy settled down, Rory-the-barista got a break from the espresso machine and came over for a chat.

"How's the writing going, Rory?" Mel asked. "Anyone ready to publish those stories you write? I sure liked that one about yoga and picking cranberries."

"Cat-Cow? Nope, no one wants that one, or any of the others. The editors send them all back," Rory said. "I think it's a crap shoot."

He ran to the counter to fill a few orders and then came back, with a chocolate-dipped biscotti for each of them and one for himself. "These are off the counter now because they are too old, but they're still perfect for dipping."

He turned to Mel. "You would not believe the stories I hear in this place when I'm doing shifts. For a writer, it's incredible, and I even get paid for it!" He was off again to tend to a customer.

When they left the café, Mel headed for his own place to pick up something he had made for Jeremy's house. As they drove through the village, Mel pointed to a house high up on the hill.

"That's where that Rex Cheever lives," he said, and he made sure Jeremy saw the house he was pointing to.

"That's a good man to stay away from. If he ever

comes to your place, you just walk out the side door and go hide in the woods until he leaves. He's no good. He's hurt a lot of people in this village one way or another, hurt them bad, especially the women. His family tries to control him but they back him up, too. You call him out for a crime and your house just might burn down. You have nothing to do with him."

They arrived at Mel's, and he opened the door to the old barn where he had his blacksmith shop. "Hard to believe I used to make a living shoeing horses," Mel said. "I used to be in here 12 hours a day. There's been no call for blacksmithing now these last 25 years, so I went clamming. Now there's a new market for hand-forged ornaments, so I'm back at it when I'm not retired. Here's one I done for you."

He picked up a two-foot steel bar with hand-hammered whales attached to it every six inches, their tails hooked upward and twisted so that each could hold up a coat. "This is for your kitchen entry way, so I'll have some place to hang my coat when I come in. What do you think?"

Jeremy ran his fingers intently over each whale, feeling the smoothness, the strength, the hardness of each curled and twisted tail, each oval body, each huge head. Then he held it out in front of him as if he were carrying a tray of crystal champagne glasses and walked back out to Mel's truck.

He cradled it in his hands on the drive back to his place and carried it carefully to the back door. He chose a location for it on the wall of the entry way and Mel put in the wood screws as Jeremy held it in place.

When the new coat rack was firmly in place, Jeremy turned to Mel and reached out for his jacket, which Mel slipped out of compliantly. Jeremy hung Mel's jacket on the first whale-tail hook, then slipped off his own jacket and hung it on the second one.

5: An urgent story

Zora sat down cautiously in the big soft armchair at one edge of Marie's kitchen, cradling her turgid breasts with one arm. "Ricky better get here quick with Bronnie, or I'll have to borrow a clean blouse and bra," she said as she settled into the chair.

"The blouse might fit," Marie replied.

As if on cue, a Lansdowne Highland pickup pulled up with a child's scream in crescendo, reaching its peak as Rick Robichaud hopped out and opened the passenger door to extract the howling Bronwyn. Three o'clock in the afternoon, a failed nap, and a long, hard day with his and Bronwyn's mutual survival as its only notable accomplishment were written all over Rick's face as he hurried in.

Bronwyn was quickly nursing, and peace reigned, at least for a while. Zora extracted a breast pump from the bag she had carried in and set to work with that as well. No milk was to be wasted; she still had calls to make that afternoon and some clinic hours in the evening.

"Jerry certainly seems to like the little cat Mel gave him," Zora commented. She had just paid the cat a professional visit, for vaccinations and a tapeworm tablet. "He's decided to call her Rosie."

Marie was startled. "He hasn't!" she exclaimed, as if truly surprised, even shocked. "Rosie?! Rose," she said softly to herself. She shook her head slightly, turned her back to the others and leaned on the kitchen counter. A moment passed before Rick and Zora realized she was crying.

"What's wrong, Marie?" Zora asked.

Marie took a deep breath and turned back to them, wiping her eyes. "That was his mother's name," she said. "Rose, Roselyn, Roselyn Parker; she was his stepmother and his legal adoptive mother. Jeremy's father used to call her Rosie. Rose was my best friend when we were growing up. Jeremy's birth mother died when he was only two years old. Rose looked after him from then on, before and after she married his dad. Rose died last year in a car accident."

"That's a lovely choice of name, then, for his sweet little cat," Zora ventured. "Is he grieving still for his stepmother?"

"It's hard to tell with Jeremy," Marie said. "Maybe his choice of name tells us something."

As they talked, Rick took the breast pump from Zora, filled two little storage bottles he'd taken from her bag and put them in Marie's fridge. He dismantled and washed up the pump and prepared a diaper change pad on a kitchen counter. "Jerry has been in this area for about as long as Zori and me," he said. "What caused him to move here, to Morganville?"

Marie scowled. "I don't usually talk about this, but maybe it's better if a few close friends know the story. Where to start?"

She said she and Rose had followed very different life paths after their girlhood together and had kept in touch only casually. Only a few months before Jeremy arrived in Morganville, Rose contacted her and said she needed her help in a big way. Up until then, Marie knew nothing of Jeremy or his family. Rose had arranged for Marie and her to meet in Toronto, in a small, windowless conference room in the Museum of Contemporary Art. She asked Marie to view the museum exhibits for at least half an hour before casually finding her way to the meeting room. It all had seemed very secretive.

Rose had an urgent story to tell. Jeremy was the younger of two children; his brother William was eight years older. William was lively and handsome and social and good at everything. By the time Jeremy was three years old, however, it was clear that he processed information and responded to people and events in unusual and atypical ways.

Different specialists classified him into different categories of mental handicap. Rose had been skeptical that these specialists really knew much that was going to be helpful to Jeremy, so with the full support of his father, she decided to take charge of his care herself. Rose was the senior vice president in a large financial firm, and she could mostly set her own rules as to where and how she worked, and they could easily pay for any help that was needed.

Jeremy seemed to thrive in activities he could do by himself and to be uncomfortable in social settings. Overall, he did well, kept up with school work and exhibited many talents.

Jeremy's father died when Jeremy was 14. Soon afterwards, his brother William proposed that Jeremy come and live with him full time, to allow them to develop a closer bond that might last into their middle and elder years.

Privately, Rose was skeptical of this plan, but Jeremy himself was enthusiastic. He worshipped his older, social and capable brother and seemed supremely happy whenever he was part of his older brother's activities. William had inherited plenty of money from his wealthy father and Jeremy would have plenty also, once he turned 21. So, with some trepidation and much personal sadness at losing her daily life with Jeremy, Rose agreed to give this a try.

All seemed to go well, but then Jeremy suddenly died about fifteen years ago, just after his fifteenth birthday. Rose described how Jeremy's body had disappeared from the crematorium and had never been recovered, and the dispute between herself and William over Jeremy's money.

One afternoon ten years later, Rose received a call on her mobile phone from a number she did not recognize. The area code was 204, Manitoba. She hesitated but then decided to answer.

A voice she did not recognize said, "Mamma Rose?"

Only one person had ever called her that.

She could hardly speak. "Julian?"—that was his real name then. "Julian? Is that you?"

"Help me Mamma Rose," the voice had said, "I ran away."

She'd had this same telephone number for almost 20 years; somehow he must have remembered it.

Jeremy was unable to explain to her where he was. She asked him to describe his surroundings and to go to the end of the block and read the street signs. From this she concluded he was in downtown Winnipeg. She learned from him that he had stolen some money and a phone. She told him to stay on that street, to go into a restaurant, to sit and eat a meal, to wait for her and that she would be there very soon. She told him to answer the phone only if it was her telephone number that was calling. He seemed to understand.

Twenty minutes later, she was in the air on her way to Winnipeg in a private jet and she found him just three hours after he had called. He was dressed in dirty torn jeans, a dirty T-shirt, a very worn leather jacket with a motorcycle insignia on the back, and black leather boots. His beard was long and untrimmed.

Rose thought they should go away somewhere immediately, away from the unknown dangers for Jeremy she felt might exist in Winnipeg and at home in Toronto. She told her pilot to take them to Quebec City and leave them there.

As they lived together in a hotel suite over the

next several days, Rose discovered that this was not the Julian she had known as a child. He was dull and slow now, with no spark at all, almost the way movie actors portray people after a frontal lobotomy.

But only almost. He seemed capable of looking after his own basic needs. In their suite, he cooked basic food, washed dishes, and was familiar with routine household tasks, as if he were used to doing them. He seemed to remember random fragments of his former life, but with no coherent story. He acted fearful and self-protective, as if he expected something bad to happen to him at every turn. He could not explain where he had been for 10 years or how he had gotten to Winnipeg. When he took off his shirt on the way to the bath, she saw that his back was scarred.

Rose had thought long and hard about what to do with Jeremy. He seemed in good physical health but to have changed mentally far beyond his childhood condition. Whatever had happened, she was sure that his brother William was behind it and might even now be looking for him again. What Jeremy needed was a place to live a good and safe life incognito, and someone to look out for him. That's when she had thought of Marie.

Marie had given up her restaurant consulting business and had moved to a house at the edge of a forest in Nova Scotia that her aunt had left to her. She had moved her dad's old mechanic shop out there and was having fun fixing old cars like she used to do with him as a child. Rose asked if she would let Jeremy live near her and keep an eye on him as needed. This was not at all Marie's concept of the free-wheeling retirement life she had in mind. She thought about it for two weeks and then said she would.

Rose had connections. She created a complete new legal identity for her son as Jeremy Franklin— passport, financial trusts, adoption record, even a convincingly official-looking but unregistered birth certificate. Only deep in the records of one investment firm and one law firm was there a paper trail to show that Jeremy Franklin and Julian Ferrante were the same person. Officially, Julian Ferrante was dead.

Jeremy Franklin was a resident of Morganville, Nova Scotia, with his own postal address, health services card, and a bank account into which a complicated and anonymous trust fund in Toronto regularly deposited a modest but decent living.

And now Rose was dead, and Marie was Jeremy's legal guardian and trustee.

There was a pause. This was an astounding story. Even Bronwyn had stopped squirming.

"I'm going to take extra special care of Rosie," Zora said.

"Marie," Rick said, "That's the strangest story I ever heard. How much of it do you think is true?"

Marie was silent for a moment. "I wondered about that myself quite often. I think the main events must be true. If Rose needed to make up a story, I don't think it would have gone like this, and Jeremy is living evidence of some sort of extraordinary past events. I can't link these main events together in any credible way, but I don't think Rose could, either. She could not really understand Jeremy's past, but she wanted to manage the future for him as best she could."

"Does Jeremy ever talk about his former life?" Zora asked.

"No. But I think more of his former self is coming back to him. Now he seems a bit more like that fourteen-year-old Rose described. Like with all the trips in the woods he's been taking with Melvin Prime this year: Mel never would have gotten him out of his house when Jeremy first arrived. Jeremy used to eat out of cans unless I fed him something better. Now he cooks regular food for himself and is even making his own bread; he actually gave a loaf to Mel as a gift! A gift to another person is a whole new concept for Jeremy."

Bronwyn made frantic motions for Rick to pick her up, and Zora gathered up her things to go out on her next call. Marie handed a travel mug of coffee to Zora as she headed out the door and poured two regular cups for herself and Rick.

Rick tickled and played with Bronwyn with suitable pauses until he was sure she was well and truly done shitting, then slung her onto the change pad, cleaned her up, greased her diaper rash from Marie's conveniently-placed butter dish and slapped on a clean diaper.

He tucked Bronwyn into the detached car seat in

which he had hurried her into the house an hour earlier. There, after some initial complaints, she fell asleep.

The timing was the worst; he could see the long late nap, long wakeful evening, late bedtime, and evaporation of his cherished few evening moments to himself, all forecast in her peaceful little face. But then she would not scream all the way home and he might get both supper and laundry done before she woke up.

He downed his coffee, grabbed Zora's milk from the fridge and hugged Marie, and he and Bronwyn were out the door.

6: The Two Felons

Rumours had been spreading that the Digby County Exhibition was going to be different this time. Attendance had been falling steadily in recent years. The ox and horse pulls remained popular, but fewer and fewer people seemed interested in the finer points of other livestock, or the top prize zucchini, or the government information brochures that were all on-line anyway. The food concession had been stuck in the age of hot dogs and fries for the last 70 years and was increasingly ignored. These days, the Ex was surviving on volunteer labour and forgiven debts.

Jimmy Prime, Mel's go-getter nephew and new president of the Ex Committee, was determined to bring back the magic. He had a plan:

- Step one: partner with the First Nation Pow Wow.
- Step two: replace the old food concession with booths run by local restaurants, cafes, breweries, and wineries, and the First Nations too, to flog their stuff and compete for customers
- Step three: get lots of other new things happening.

Jimmy had wheedled and annoyed Rick and Zora into inventing, making and selling zany and only-at-the-Ex ice cream from their usual Lansdowne Highland Cheese booth at the fair. They had resisted at first, but had had fun coming up with a rhubarb-ginger-beet ice cream of exquisite colour, a cranberry-raspberry-maple sugar crunch, and a sticky vanilla cream ripple studded with cherries, which Jimmy had insisted they call 'sex ice cream' and which sold out on the first day.

A local club of medievalists were holding combat demonstrations, including full-on jousting on galloping Percherons. There was a 'biathlon booth' at which people could pay to shoot at a target with a space-age biathlon competition rifle and live ammunition, and there was to be a special marksmanship demonstration, a featured event for the Saturday afternoon, just before the finalist horse and ox pulls and the night of big Pow Wow dance competitions.

Somewhat against his will, Rick found himself at the Ex on that Saturday afternoon, waiting for the shooting show. Rick had no interest in guns or shooting. However, Melvin Prime had insisted unremittingly for the past two weeks that Rick and Zora just had to come to this show. Mel would not explain why; he said it had to be a secret until the show, but he was so determined that they could not say no.

Zora was the vet in attendance for the day anyway, so she could be there if no animal injuries kept her away. The time of day annoyed Rick. It was fully in the range of Bronwyn's afternoon nap. Fortunately, today Bronnie had gone down early and woken up in time on her own, and had eaten well before they had to leave for the Ex.

A big crowd had gathered for the shooting show by the time Rick and Bronwyn arrived. Mel must have been persuasive with others, too, because Marie and Lisa were there, neither of whom, Rick was sure, had any interest in this sort of thing.

Zora ran up at the last minute and snatched Bronwyn for a rare afternoon snuggle. Mel had fetched Jeremy for the show, too, and was standing with him right in the middle of the front row.

Out in front of that first row was a table on which there was a rifle, some boxes of shells and various other objects. Three of the five-target biathlon target frames stood about 150 feet out in the field in front of the audience and there was a vertical wooden frame of some sort off to one side from which small objects were dangling.

A TV reporter and cameraman were strategically placed nearby and Constable Roger Laliberty, the Mountie who had lived in Bear River for the past six years, stood at one end of the front row, because the event involved shooting live ammunition.

At the appointed time, Jimmy Prime walked out into the field in front of the crowd with a portable microphone. "Ladies and gentlemen," he proclaimed, "You are about to witness an historic event, the first time that marksmanship of such exceptional skill has been seen in Digby County since the days of Mr.

Henry Albert Pattinson Smith, the Sheriff of Digby County 120 years ago. Sheriff Smith was a sharp-shooter of international renown, and used his prodigious marksmanship to garner respect among the righteous and to inspire fear among criminals. He went to fairs and exhibitions to demonstrate his skills and today you are about to witness some of those same tricks of shooting that made Sheriff Smith so famous in his day. Ladies and gentlemen, it is my honour now to present to you a marksman fully in the tradition Sheriff Smith himself, Bear River and Morganville's own Mr. Jeremy Franklin!"

There was a loud cheer from the crowd, almost none of whom had any idea who Jeremy Franklin was. On the faces of the few who did, there was only bewilderment.

Mel and Jeremy stood up and walked to the table, where they fumbled momentarily with the rifle and the shells.

Jimmy Prime called to the crowd, "Who among you tried your hand shooting at the biathlon booth?" About 30 or 40 hands waived in the air. "How many of you hit at least one of the five targets with your ten shots?" About a dozen or so hands remained in the air. "Two targets?" One lone hand waived and there was a little burst of applause for such good shooting.

"Jeremy," Jimmy said, "show us how it's done!"

It seemed to Rick that Jeremy was not paying any attention to Jimmy or to the crowd, but was listening to Mel beside him. He picked up the rifle, an old pump .22, stepped away from the table and stood on a small piece of carpet that marked the point 150 feet from the 15 targets, each one just under 2 inches in diameter. He put the gun to his shoulder, pointed it at the target furthest to the right, and started shooting quickly but not hurriedly.

Bang-pump, bang-pump, bang-pump...

Fifteen shots, and fifteen targets flashed from black to white, one after another: a perfect score.

The crowd sat in stunned silence for a long five seconds, and then exploded into wild cheers and applause.

Mel brought Jeremy back to the table while Jimmy, helped by Constable Laliberty, carried the wooden frame out to a position in front of the crowd and placed it on a ground cloth about 50 feet from the shooter's mat. The top bar of the frame was ten feet off the ground. Five pieces of thin, clothesline-style rope each suspended an empty wine bottle about six inches below the top bar.

"Sheriff Smith called this next trick 'The Two Felons'," Jimmy told the crowd.

Mel spoke to Jeremy and he went out to the shooter's mat again. He aimed and fired two shots in rapid succession: *bang-pump-bang.*

The first shot snapped the rope holding the centre-most wine bottle and the second shot broke the bottle before it had reached the ground.

Without pausing, Jeremy repeated this trick four times, then came back to Mel at the table.

Again, here was a pause, and then the crowd again

went wild.

Jimmy Prime now tied a length of rope about six feet long to the centre of the upper bar and attached a double-size full bottle of top-quality rye whisky to its lower end. He pulled the bottle off to one side and let it swing across the space beneath the bar like a pendulum.

He turned to the crowd. "Sheriff Smith was once asked to shoot and destroy a new, full bottle of whisky as a statement in favour of temperance," he said. "But his hard-drinking old friend and hunting partner came up to him and asked him please to shoot the rope instead and spare the whisky. So now it's up to you. Jeremy is going to blast all that good whisky away unless one of you is willing to pay enough money for him to change his mind. The money goes to the food bank and the whisky to the generous high bidder, but you had better bid lots or that whisky's gone. Who's got the first bid?" As Jimmy worked the crowd for bids, Mel took Jeremy to the shooter's mat and then went to the wooden frame.

Mel gave the bottle a hard push so it would swing in a wide arc and then moved quickly away. Jeremy put the gun to his shoulder and began tracking the bottle.

"Twenty-five dollars," someone shouted. *Bang.* The shot missed.

"That was a warning shot," Jimmy scolded. "You're never going to low-ball Jeremy."

"$50 dollars." *Bang.*

"I think that almost grazed the label," Jimmy said. "Who's got a real bid?"

"One hundred dollars," someone cried. *Bang*.

This time Jeremy had aimed the gun a bit high and away from the target with an abrupt motion.

Mel signalled to Jeremy, who lowered his gun while Mel got the bottle swiftly swinging again

"Getting better," Jimmy said.

"$150." *Bang*.

"$175." *Bang*.

"$225." *Bang*.

"$275." *Bang*.

Somebody finally shouted, "$300!"

Now there was another pause.

Bang.

The rope snapped and the whisky bottle dropped to a soft landing on the ground cloth.

"Mitchell Puddister is today's most generous man," Jimmy cried.

The crowd roared. Mitchell ran down to Jimmy, cheque book in hand, and ran back the proud owner of Digby County's most famous bottle of whisky.

Mel helped Jeremy reload the rifle and moved the shooter's mat off to one side, to be even with the edge of the audience area and facing at an angle across the shooting space. Mel went back to the table and picked up a small pail while Jimmy Prime got on the microphone again.

"Folks, you know Mel here has been helping out with this show, but now he's really pissed off. He says your pitiful cheers wouldn't be enough to praise a tomcat for his kittens and it's just an insult to the likes of Jeremy. So Mel's going to give you what he thinks you deserve and they're right there in that little pail of his."

Mel was about forty feet out in front of the crowd. Now he spun around, glowering, and shouted, "Here's for you, you ungrateful bunch of jam tarts."

His pail was half full of raw eggs. He grabbed one and lobbed it high into the air on a trajectory for the middle of the crowd.

There was a collective scream and scramble away from the impact site and immediately the bang of the rifle. The egg disintegrated in the air high over Mel's head.

He grabbed another and lobbed it at the audience and Jeremy shot it out of the air again.

The audience screamed less at the third egg and less again at the fourth. By the time Jeremy had destroyed the fifteenth egg, their consternation had turned into the roar of a hometown crowd watching their own team heading unstoppably toward a winning goal.

As the final five eggs were thrown and destroyed, the audience united in a group chant: "Jerry! Jerry! Jerry!" They didn't know who he was, but he sure could shoot.

After the last egg was shot away, Mel turned his pail upside down high up in the air to show it was empty and the show was over. As the crowd started to disperse, Jeremy turned his back to them, pumped his next-to-last .22 shell high in the air, and blew it away with his last shot.

The TV reporter wanted to talk to Jeremy, but Mel said it wasn't possible, that he was too shy to be interviewed, so the reporter ran after Jimmy Prime instead. Marie, Lisa, Rick and Zora stood together now, half dumbfounded, half frightened by what they had just witnessed. Bronwyn had paid no attention to any of it.

Rick ran off and returned with two big bowls of beet ice cream for the shooter and his assistant. Mel looked at Marie with an expression that was half coyote, half sheep and asked, "Did you know he could do that?"

"I did not," Marie said, a touch icily. "How did you know?"

"At camp," Mel said. "I couldn't believe it. You just can't keep this kind of thing a secret."

Marie turned to Jeremy. "Jerry, where did you learn to shoot?"

"Don't know," was all he would reply, looking away.

Bronwyn had not recognized Jeremy during the event, but now, when she heard his voice, she made frantic gestures toward him and Zora handed her over.

Jeremy and Bronwyn both seemed to relax, which caused everyone else to relax, too. It all had been kind of intense.

Jeremy walked in a small circle, bouncing Bronwyn along ever so slightly as he went. Then paused, hugged her just a little more, looked down at the ground in Marie's general direction, and said, "Fergus."

"I gotta go, Ricky," Zora said. "There's one horse in the next pull I said can't go in unless his foot swelling has gone way down. They'll be harnessing up in a few minutes. Let's just each grab some supper here tonight, save you some work at home?"

Zora looked him in the eyes, gave him a quick kiss, and hustled off to the horse barn. Some volunteers were cleaning up the ground cloth and broken glass.

Rick collected Bronwyn from Jeremy, loaded her into the carrying sling and went off toward the booths to forage for a meal. Mel and Jeremy gathered up the rifle, pail and shells from the table and took a short cut out to Mel's truck through a hole in the back fence to avoid the general crowd. Marie and Lisa just stood together for a while, watching them go.

~

It had been a slow day in the world of TV news and, across the country, many stations were pleased to pick up and broadcast a diverting account of a display of marksmanship at a country fair in Nova Scotia. The editors had zeroed in particularly on the auction of the bottle of whisky and the eggs threatening to rain down on the crowd, protected by a sharp-shooting lone ranger seen mostly from the back and at some distance.

William Ferrante watched this unexpected TV

side story with unusual attention and accelerating rage. He had known a person who could shoot like that, his brother. But that brother was as good as dead, and his name was not Jeremy Franklin.

Ferrante watched the clip again, tracking the shooter, his mechanical bearing, his indifference to the audience, his emotion-free speed and precision. Waves of anger, of outrage at the injustices he suffered and the humiliation of being deceived, swept him into the vortex of his paranoia.

He threw his beer bottle into the TV screen and ran to the drawer where he kept his pay-as-you-go untraceable phone.

7: Come ASAP

The day at the Ex was over, concluded by a good supper of Pow Wow bannock and smoked meat, muskeg tea and a bowl of sex ice cream the staff at the Lansdowne Highland Cheese booth had saved for Rick. Now it was bedtime.

Bedtime with Bronwyn sometimes brought to Rick that same sense of vast and incomprehensible delight that a night sky full of stars can inspire, but more often it was just a trial, cuddling the beloved child while wishing desperately for release from her and for a few moments of personal freedom. It was a time of day when conflicting thoughts and emotions sometimes were churned up to the surface. Had he abandoned a career as a hot shot scientist for this? No, he had abandoned that career for Zora. Everything else had just happened along the way, including Bronwyn. Zora had swept him up, like a feather in a tornado.

"Hi, I'm Rick Robichaud, your lab instructor."

"Hi." Then, "Hey wait, Rick Robichaud? Really? from Westport? I beat your ass in the debate club provincials five years ago; do you remember? I was on the team from St Mary's Bay Academy. Zora Cromwell." And she had shaken his hand.

Rick had looked at her then with full attention. She really had beat his ass, the little black girl in dreadlocks with the best speech in the competition. But there had been some changes. She had become the most beautiful woman in the world.

She asked, "What are you doing here at McGill?"

"Fish ecology. How about you?"

"I'm in vet school at St-Hy, just taking this course for interest. I'm working on campus for the summer, so its free."

They'd gone out for a beer after that first lab, to talk about their homes and friends in western Nova Scotia. They moved in together four weeks later and lived that way for the next three years.

During her last term of vet school, as graduation was approaching, Zora had become increasingly anxious. One night it had all come out in a flood of tears. "Ricky, I want to be with you forever, but I can't. I have to be a vet, I just *have* to. Ever since I was old enough to know what it was, I've had to be a vet. And I have to go back and be a vet where I grew up, where we grew up, and help make things better there. I just have to. But you can't go there; it wouldn't be fair to you. There is nothing for you to do there. There's no life for a top scientist in Weymouth Falls or anywhere near by. I want you to have the life you've earned. I can't take that away from you."

They had cried themselves to sleep. Three days later, he withdrew from his PhD program. "I'm coming with you," he told Zora that evening. "We'll make it work."

Rick's phone vibrated silently: a text from Zora.

She should have been the one putting Bronwyn to bed right now, but an emergency call had come in and a client had rushed some ailing animal to the clinic at the back of the house.

Bronwyn seemed mostly asleep, so Rick took the chance, gently extracted his phone and looked at the message: "Need help; come ASAP"

As Soon As Possible is a fantasy when it comes to babies, but maybe, just maybe, Bronwyn would stay asleep when he put her in her crib. It was worth a try.

He rose with every muscle tensed for smoothness, leaned deeply into the crib to lay Bronwyn on the mattress before loosening any part of his body contact with her. He detached himself on a slow count to 30 and stood still to assess the result.

After a few squirms and one alarming flash of open eyes, Bronwyn relaxed into unhurried regular breathing. Rick switched on the baby monitor, stepped out the door, booted up his baby monitor app, watched Bronwyn on his phone screen for 30 seconds more, and raced for the clinic.

Two cats were on the examination table. Zora had put a breathing tube into a big, long-haired tortoise-shell and was rhythmically squeezing an air bag to breathe for the animal. "Ricky, can you take over here? You have to breathe for this cat. Push in about a half cup of air very gently and let the chest's recoil push it out. Count slow seconds and give her a breath every 2-3."

Zora turned her attention to the other cat, a black

and white short-hair which was still breathing on its own, but was not moving. Like the tortoiseshell, its eyelids were wide open, never blinking, eyes not moving.

Zora put drops in both cats' eyes from time to time as she examined the less-affected cat. The cats' owner sat in a chair not far from the table, watching carefully and looking worried.

"I'm sorry, Mrs. Schreiber," Zora said. "I haven't been able properly to talk to you about the cats or tell you what I am doing. This is my husband, Rick. Now let's go back to the beginning."

Mrs. Schreiber said that the cats had suddenly started moving in abnormal ways, with a very odd gait, and licking their lips and paws oddly at the same time. They had seemed to lose coordination first in their hind legs, then the front legs. The tortoiseshell had collapsed about an hour ago.

The Schreibers were renting a house at Rossway for a few weeks and they had just moved in. Their veterinarian in New Jersey had determined that the tortoiseshell cat, Mildred, had an enlarged heart and had prescribed a daily dose of canned clams to correct a nutrient deficiency she thought might be the cause.

Mrs. Schreiber had not found canned clams in the local grocery store, but a neighbour had urged her just to go out at low tide and dig some, which, with some instruction, she had done. She had fed the clams to the cats that evening, giving Mildred the lion's share. All other aspects of the cats' lives had been the usual routine. They were indoor cats, never allowed outside.

"What do you think is wrong?" she asked.

Zora said, "I think it may be shellfish poisoning."

She explained that she had never seen a case before but had learned about it in vet school, but mainly about its effect on people. A toxin produced by tiny algae in the ocean that the clams eat causes it. The toxin could build up in clams to poisonous levels and it paralyzed muscles. Zora thought Mildred's breathing muscles were paralyzed like her leg muscles.

The black and white cat had started to blink its eyes occasionally, and Zora thought that this was a sign that it was recovering. She did not know whether Mildred would survive. Artificial breathing was the only way to keep animals and people alive when breathing muscles become paralyzed. "We have to continue breathing for her until the effects of the toxin wear off. That could be in a few hours or in a few days."

"Do you think I could do the breathing for Mildred?" Mrs. Schreiber asked. "You can't keep doing this all night or for days on end, but maybe my husband and I could."

Zora said it was possible and gave Mrs. Schreiber a quick lesson. "Really, you know, no one is very skilled at this," she said. "No one does this very often. You likely can do it as well as any veterinarian, but you will need someone to spell you off from time to time. It is quite tiring."

The black and white cat was starting to move its legs, and Zora declared it to be out of danger.

"If you can keep Mildred breathing, I can drive you home," Rick said. "You can come back for your car another day."

It was only a 20-minute drive to Rossway. As Rick and Mrs. Schreiber prepared to leave, Zora said, "If Mildred starts to recover, you'll have to remove the breathing tube. Take the clamp off that tiny little rubber tube on the side and then pull the whole thing out, gently but all in one motion if you can. Don't take it out until Mildred starts to retch just a little. That's the signal. She will be able to breathe on her own if she can retch."

They installed Mrs. Schreiber in the passenger seat with Mildred and the breathing apparatus in her lap, and put the other cat in a box on the floor. Mr. Schreiber was waiting when they arrived, ready to do his part.

Rick wished them well and headed back home.

The next morning, the Schreibers returned, bringing with them the body of Mildred, who had died about 3 am.

"Her heart just seemed to stop," Mrs. Schreiber said sadly.

"I am so sorry," Zora said. "And I am sorry to ask this of you now, but will you let me do an autopsy to make sure my clinical assessment was correct?"

The Schreibers agreed, waited an hour for Zora to do what she had to do, and then took Mildred back home to bury. They thanked Zora for her hard work.

Zora had found nothing abnormal in Mildred's body, which ruled out many different diseases but did not really confirm the poisoning. She had found some bits of clam in the cat's stomach and had saved these to test for toxins, but she was not sure she could find a laboratory that would test them.

As a starting point, she called an acquaintance who worked on the food safety side of the provincial Department of Fisheries. He said the Department probably would not agree to test an autopsy sample from a cat, but he said the entire northeast half of St Mary's Bay had been closed to shellfish harvest for the past four weeks due to very high levels of these shellfish toxins.

"You don't have to test any clams taken recently near Rossway to see if they have enough toxin to kill a cat," he said. "They do."

8: I won't need these for long

Wiss Artinian's phone rang twice and then stopped. Then it rang four times and stopped and then three times.

He grabbed it and shouted, "That's the old code, you fucking asshole. Who the fuck is this?"

Wiss was at his usual place of business, twenty feet underground in the bunker of the C Company Motor Cycle Club compound in north Winnipeg, at the end of an average day. He was still running the last bit of his evening heroin into a vein and he did not appreciate this interruption. Nobody called Wiss; Wiss called you.

"Where's Julian, you cock-sucker?"

The voice was ever so slightly familiar, but Wiss couldn't place it. "Who the fuck is Julian?"

"You stupid son-of-a-bitch, he's the kid whose not-really-dead body I paid you big bucks to steal, to feed drugs, and to take into your sick-o bunker family as handy cheap labour. Where is he?"

"The kid? Bimbo? He hasn't been here for years. I don't know where the fuck he is, and I don't give a shit."

"I paid you two hundred thousand to give a shit

for as long as he lived, you cunt, and ten thousand a year on top of that. Start remembering. Where did he go?"

"I don't know where the fuck he went. One day he was here, next day he wasn't. Must'a just walked out one day when we weren't locked down. Probably died on the street. Fuck him, who cares?"

"You had better start caring in a hurry. When did he leave?"

"When? How the fuck do I know when? Years ago."

"You've been taking my payments for Julian for years and him not even there, and not a word to me? C Company had better be doing extra well these days because you've got a hell of a debt to pay."

"I got no debt to you, fuckhead. When Bimbo was here, he was a useless tit, 24/7. He was brain dead. Had to hit him just to get him to clean the bathroom. If it had been up to me, he'd 'a been down the garburator long ago. But the girls wanted to keep him, said he was cute. They liked to fuck him and make him cry. Your money never covered half of the trouble he was to me."

"Wiss, there's a guy here in Toronto who would really enjoy skinning you alive, just to feel your pain and watch you die. He's cheap, because of the enjoyment factor. There's another with enough gelignite to blow you and your useless bunker into the middle of Lake Winnipeg. He's cheap, too, loves the big bang. You had better put a lot of cash in some boxes right now and hide them away until I find you again. When I do, it won't be a phone call. You'll just feel all these little taser needles dig into you, and then you'll wake up lying on a floor somewhere, unable to move, listening to a knife being sharpened."

Ferrante sent his phone crashing into the wall across the room. What a fuckup! How quickly could he catch and slowly kill Wiss Artinian?

Night was gradually descending on the town of Fergus. The late summer evenings were bringing cool air now as a respite from the daytime heat. The loud roar of the air conditioner was annoying Ferrante and confusing his thoughts, so he turned it off and opened some windows.

Wiss must have planned this all from the beginning. Maybe he had not even given Julian the LSD and the Datura seeds and the beatings after he stole the body. Maybe Wiss had turned on him, maybe he'd even sent Julian to the police.

Ferrante was too angry to think. He packed his steam-roller with Fordnation Gold and took 4 long, deep tokes. Retribution for the plots Wiss Artinian had raised against him gradually began to seem less urgent. This could wait.

The immediate problem was Julian, whom he had just seen alive on TV despite being among the walking dead for the last 15 years, and Julian's inheritance, which was rightfully his. Ferrante had never wanted to kill Julian, only to make him disappear.

Now, it seemed, Julian had escaped from that benevolent plan and was living somewhere in Nova Scotia under an assumed name, perhaps plotting even now some form of revenge.

As the THC brought clarity to his thoughts, Ferrante realized that his first action must be to find Julian, regain control of him, get to his inheritance, and put him away for good. Roselyn was dead now; it should be easy.

The non-stop ringing of his personal phone awakened him. It was 10 o'clock in the morning, and the sun streaming in the window hurt his eyes.

The phone displayed Randall's number, a business partner in Winnipeg, so he answered. "What do you want, Randall? I got enough on my plate without you adding anything more."

"You been talking to Wiss Artinian?"

"Who wants to know?"

"Don't get cute with me, Ferrante. I'm only calling because I got investments in your ass. Did you piss off Wiss somehow? Word is that C Company is getting ready to ride and they're headed for you. You don't want to be there when they arrive."

"Those assholes owe me big-time. They should be riding in the opposite direction, trying to hide."

"Stop dreaming, Ferrante. They'll burn everything you own and throw you into the fire when you're only half dead. Get out of town today and stay hid for a few years."

"I'm leaving for a better reason. I was going to call you anyway. I need a good ID, all the papers. What do we have in stock?"

There was a pause as Randall looked something up on his computer. "How about Billy Cleveland? Your age, died on the street because of a little crossfire, no family or address. We got the SIN number and birth certificate. I can match up a health card and driver's license, too. What province?"

"Nova Scotia. I won't need these for long, and when I'm done with this business, I'll have a few surprises for Wiss Artinian."

"Where do I send the papers?"

Billy checked a map of Nova Scotia on his phone. "Send them to me at General Delivery in Windsor, Nova Scotia. Express post."

"Is your house insured?"

"I'm renting."

"Get your stuff out of there today and don't be there tonight."

Randall was gone.

~

The young lady running the night shift at the Windsor motel had been enthusiastic in bed but wasn't willing to risk her job by staying away from her desk for another hour. It was too early for sleep, so Ferrante fired up his laptop and started to contemplate how best to start his search.

It was Tuesday. He had seen the news clip of Julian sharpshooting on Saturday night. The country fair somewhere in Nova Scotia, where Julian had made the news, probably was over.

He made a search of fairs in Nova Scotia that weekend and there had been only one: the Digby County Exhibition at Bear River, 150 miles away to the west, right down Highway 101. Easy to find, probably easy to get people to talk about the shooting show and who the shooter was. Maybe he even lived nearby.

But Ferrante began to worry. This all could be a trap, a trap for him. They could have staged that shooting show just to get it on the TV news to lure him in. Wiss Artinian might be using Julian as bait to get him away from his guys in Toronto. Maybe Randall was in on it too; probably he was.

He had better be careful. Better not go right to Bear River. Better to disguise himself, hang out in the area, watch things from a distance, get social with the right people, slowly move in closer.

The old Jeep he'd bought was a good start, licensed to Billy Cleveland of Windsor, NS. He needed a week to grow enough of a beard to change his face. He would spend a day exploring Windsor for background, tour Cape Breton and spend some days in Halifax. Then he would rent a place not too close, in Digby maybe or in Annapolis Royal. From there he could set his net and slowly close it around Julian.

Ferrante's lawyer in Toronto had been clear. As far as the law was concerned, Julian was dead, and his estate was settled.

It would take a very alive and compliant Julian Ferrante to convince the law otherwise, or a truly dead Jeremy Franklin whose real identity would come to light eventually and cause enough legal confusion to open up the inheritance case again, with no one left to contest it.

9: No place for people like you

Zora squatted down in front the big old ox where he lay on the ground beside his barn in the soft morning light. She rubbed the crown of his head between his horns with a few firm scratching strokes.

"Bright is never going to stand up again Mr. Polder," she said. "I think you have made the right decision."

Harold Polder was standing beside Zora, looking haggard. "Yes," he said, in a tone of resigned despair, "Please."

He paused for a moment, then turned and walked quickly out of sight around the barn.

Zora stroked Bright once more, then gently traced a line through his hair with her finger from right ear to left eye and then from left ear to right eye. She twirled her finger in his hair at the point where the two lines crossed in the middle of his forehead, then stepped back, aimed her shotgun at the spot, and pulled the trigger.

In the few moments of silence that followed, Zora felt the intense waves of sadness and relief that always swept over her at such times. She had just destroyed a magnificent animal, but she also had put an end to intense suffering and spared a man the pain of himself having to end the life of his companion of 15 years. She had done the same for Bright's teammate, Lion, the year before, and for the same reasons.

The sound of an engine starting up broke the spell. Harold Polder came around the corner of the barn, driving a front-end loader with an array of ropes, wooden beams, knives and saws in the bucket. He stopped behind Bright and turned off the engine.

"Thank you, Dr. Cromwell," he said. "Don't nobody around here like to kill his own cattle. Years ago, we used to do it for each other, but there's hardly anyone around has cattle now. I can carry on from here. Will you come back and look at the meat after? It's worth it to me if you will."

Zora said she would come back about 4 pm and reminded Harold what he needed to save for her to see in order to do a proper health inspection.

She took the two unused shells out of the gun, ran a rag through the barrel to clean it and threw the shotgun behind the seat of her truck. Three more calls to do before her lunch-time rendezvous with Ricky and Bronnie in Bear River. She was off.

Bronwyn was down for the count, a morning nap that might just last a full two hours. Rick had gotten a cassoulet into the slow cooker and a load of diapers into the washer and had made it to La Fromagerie for the staff meeting. He sat there feeling like a school child participating in the annual spend-a-day-with-your-parent-at-work program. He knew the least of anyone at the table. The staff were on about switching to fall feed and managing the impact of silage on milk flavour.

Crazy Uncle Gilles had invented all of this. At age 40, he'd gambled and won, Chased the Ace at Meteghan fire hall, took the $4 million jackpot, splurged on a trip to Europe, seen highland cattle for the first time and fallen in love, decided he could double his money by making cheese from their milk as a niche commodity back home, bought all the farmland in Lansdowne and had done it. His mother's crazy brother, who'd never had a real job anyone in his family could recognize.

His little farm and fromagerie was turning over $3 million a year now. He'd put together the best registered Highlands in the country, could sell even the runtiest bull calf for $10,000. He employed 15 people full-time and they all got benefits and profit shares; he had paid himself about the same as he paid them.

Then he'd gotten phlebitis in his legs, and the pain was too much for him. He could not imagine going through all the surgeries and he went out among his cows one afternoon and shot himself.

And he'd left the whole thing to Rick, of all people, every last fence post and hay bale, to his crazy nephew Rick who had walked away from a big university career to come home.

A wail from the baby monitor app interrupted Rick's little personal retrospective.

"Bronnie's hungry, Daddy-o," Edgar, the cheese guru, remarked. "By the way, Marie was right, that cheese stall in Montreal wants all of that new cheese we can send them. They want a good name for it, too. How about 'Highland Bronnie's Triple Scream'?"

There were giggles all around the table.

"How about everyone comes up with two names and we figure it out next week?" Rick said, as he ran out the door for the house.

Bronwyn had awakened in fine form, guzzling all her milk and interested in Rick's slice of bread (allowed) and coffee (not allowed). Rick put her in the stroller, gave her a chunk of bread as a distraction and got all the diapers on the clothesline before she started to fuss for new entertainment.

Rick was way ahead of her. The stroller was the kind intended for runners. He already had loaded it with the travelling baby gear and the mail from Lansdowne Highland, and was ready to get some real exercise running Bronwyn down to meet Zora for lunch in Bear River.

It was mostly down hill, but it was a good run even so. Bronwyn always was happiest at high speed, which was strong incentive to keep up a good pace.

They zigzagged a bit at the Bear River end to avoid some dangerous curves and came to a halt on the flat by the post office, right on schedule.

As Rick was sorting out the mail and getting ready to carry Bronwyn into the post office with him, Millie Cheever came skipping across the street from the general store. Millie was an eager eight-year-old and a favourite with Bronwyn. She leaned over the stroller, talking and tickling, and Bronwyn laughed and laughed and waited for more.

"Millie," Rick asked, "do you want to stay here with Bronnie while I run into the post office?"

"Oh, yes!" Millie said.

Rick gathered up the mail and went inside.

The street in front of the general store was the gathering place for locals who wanted to smoke while drinking their coffee. As Rick disappeared into the post office, Rex Cheever emerged from this group and crossed the street to Bronwyn and Millie. When Millie saw him approaching, she quickly moved to the handles of the stroller and began pushing it away toward the post office entrance.

Rex halted her progress with one foot.

Millie placed herself between Rex and Bronwyn. "You leave her alone, Uncle Rex," she said, a mix of determination and fear in her voice.

"Stand aside, Millie," Rex said, "I just want to have a look at this thing."

He leaned in over Bronwyn and made a slight grimace. "Isn't that just ugly," he said, mostly to himself.

He raised his head and shouted across the street, "Eugene, George, come look at this."

Two men, one walking with a cane, detached themselves from the group and walked over to Rex.

"What you got there, Rex?" one said, "Is that a bear or a monkey? I seen curly black hair like that on a bear cub I shot one time."

All three now glared down at Bronwyn.

"Whatever it is," Rex said, "it ain't human."

He picked up a few small stones from the road and tossed one into the stroller, missing Bronwyn. He tossed in another that hit her on the head, and she began to cry.

Millie grabbed the stroller handles and tried to wheel it away from the men, but Rex grabbed her by one arm and threw her to the ground. "Gimme that cane, Eugene, see if I can make it wiggle."

He took the cane and started poking Bronwyn in the stomach. Millie ran toward the post office screaming, "Mr. Robichaud!"

Rick and the postmistress heard Millie's scream and looked out the window. Rick was through the door before Millie could reach it, racing for the stroller.

He pushed the men roughly aside, picked up the wailing Bronwyn and held her close against him. He spun around to face the men. Eugene and George looked down at the ground and started moving away; only Rex held his gaze.

"What the hell are you doing?" Rick yelled. He could just barely contain his rage.

"Ain't no place around here for people like you" Rex growled. "Don't you come here no more. You're a disgrace."

He suddenly swung the cane in a blow aimed at

Rick's head. Rick turned away and ducked. The cane struck a glancing blow on the back of his head, knocking him down on one knee as he kept his embrace of Bronwyn.

Rex stepped forward and struck Rick again, a blow to the shoulders and another across the back. As he raised his cane high for a heavier blow, there was a loud explosion directly behind him that stopped him in mid-swing. He turned quickly around to see what it was.

Rex found himself staring up the still-smoking barrel of a shotgun into the steel gaze of Dr. Zora Cromwell.

She pumped a new shell into the chamber with a clatter of metal levers and set her finger firmly against the trigger. In the fray around the baby stroller, no one had noticed her truck pull up in front of the store.

"You trying to kill my husband with a club while he's saving his baby, Rex Cheever?" Zora's voice was as quiet and steady as her aim at the middle of Rex's forehead, but seething also, like an electric wire charged with 10,000 volts. She flicked off the safety latch with her thumb, ready to fire again.

Rick was on the ground bleeding, still holding the hysterical child. Rex and everyone else stood paralyzed.

"Don't kill him, Zora." It was Becky Cheever, Millie's mother. She had stepped out of the store and was walking toward Zora and Rex in slow measured steps. "This community needs you alive more than we need Rex dead. If there was real justice around here, they'd have locked Rex up long ago, but there isn't. There's only the law of the land that people won't use and clans looking after themselves. If you shoot Rex, you'll be locked up for years. You don't owe us that sacrifice."

She had reached Zora by this time and she gently put her hand on the gun barrel and pushed it slowly upward, away from an aim at anything.

Then she turned to Rex with her face crimson with anger. She grabbed the cane which he still held in his hand and hit him such a powerful blow to the head that he crumpled to his knees.

"You're a sick weak coward, Rex Cheever," she yelled at him. "The family says we can manage you, but they know we can't. You do nothing but hurt people. If it was me holding that gun, you'd be a dead man." She threw the cane aside.

Zora pumped the last live shell out of the gun chamber and ran to Rick and Bronwyn, crying, hugging, inspecting wounds, pulling Millie in to see if Rex had hurt her also.

In the drama of the past few minutes, few had noticed the arrival of Constable Roger Laliberty in front of the post office. The post mistress had called the police. Roger's training told him to intervene immediately, side arm drawn, but he hesitated.

When Zora disarmed her gun and ran to her family, Roger strode forward, silencing the crowd with the possibility of further drama. He could only guess what had happened before his arrival, but he was confidant that he knew where justice lay and what parts of the law of the land could be applied to achieve it, even if only temporarily.

He walked over to Rex Cheever, who was just getting to his feet, put him in handcuffs, and marched him to the patrol car.

10: No brother

Rory had learned a few things about rural life since he and Lisa had come to Bear River a few years ago. One was never to attend community "public inform- ation meetings." Out of a sense of civic duty and curi- osity, he had gone to one such meeting last year, put on by the volunteer fire department, and somehow he had left that meeting a volunteer fire fighter, with weekly training meetings and always on call.

Now here he was, heading home from a late morning grass fire at Cornwallis Park, steering the old pumper truck back to the station, taking the long, slow way around to avoid going down the steep hills. He had developed a deep sense of belonging and fellowship with this wonderful group of fire fighters and valued every minute he spent with them, but he was missing his weekly coffee club. If he was lucky, he might just catch the last half hour.

The coffee club had been Lisa's idea, an hour every Thursday afternoon when they and their friends would converge on the café and catch up with each other. They all would just wrangle their schedules somehow and make it happen.

Underneath Lisa's genuine and thick outer layer

of sweetness was a dynamo that powered many things, including unmatched persuasion. Rory worked at the café Thursday afternoons anyway; usually there was not a lot of business then, and he could join in, at the table or from behind the counter. Zora and Rick could get there most weeks and so could four or five others.

It was a highlight of the week for all of them and Rory was vexed that he was going to miss it. As he rolled into the fire station, he was delighted to find that several other volunteers were ready to take over and recharge everything. He quickly took off his protective suit and ran to the café.

Conversation was in full swing when he arrived, and Rory's boss, who had minded the shop while Rory was off fighting the fire, told him to take a break and join the group.

Monica Jeffries, one of Rory's sometime co-workers, motioned him over to her before he could sit down. Beside her was a man Rory did not recognize. "Rory, I want you to meet Billy Cleveland. We're kind of hanging out together these days, so I brought him along."

"So glad to meet you, Billy. Welcome to the group," Rory said, shaking his hand warmly.

This seemed like an uptick for Monica, a really fine person who had not done so well lately in the romance department. Monica lived and worked in Annapolis Royal but did some shifts at the café counter too. Billy looked about ten years older than Monica, but it was hard to tell through his dense

Ted Leighton

black beard.

Rory pulled a chair up beside Henry, the English-professor-turned-songwriter, and they immediately got into to a favourite topic: Walt Whitman.

Lisa was cuddling Bronwyn and Rick was enjoying a few moments in his own space. He wondered who Monica's new boyfriend was. He seemed nice enough, very amiable and social. Rick did not know Monica all that well, but she seemed to him to be emotionally fragile, easily misled and easily hurt, very giving and loving, perhaps to a fault. He hoped the new guy would feel and honour her goodness and treat her well.

Rick leaned across the table. "Hello, Billy, I'm Rick, Rick Robichaud. Zora and Bronwyn and I live just up the hill in Lansdowne. Zora's a vet; Bronnie and I run a farm. What brings you to Western Nova Scotia?"

Billy said he had moved here from southern Ontario just three weeks ago. He was renting a place in Annapolis Royal and soon would be looking a-round for some kind of work.

Monica added, "Ricky looks after Bronwyn FULL-TIME!"

They all smiled, and Monica and Billy went back to conversations closer to their seats.

Rick wondered, *Do I really look after Bronwyn full time? Is that all I do?* A month ago, when Zora had first gone back to work, sometimes it had seemed that way. Now though, he didn't think it was true. It was more like he and Bronnie were a team and to-gether they got a lot done.

Who took care of whom? He organized their jobs and she organized their days. They certainly never slept in or wasted time. Together they ran the farm. They were yoked together like oxen, that was for sure, but did one of them really pull harder than the other? Bronwyn set the pace, and they pulled the load together. They laughed and cried together by turns; he'd be lost without her.

Lisa rose, handed Bronwyn to Zora. "I have to be off."

On her way out, she called to Rory, "I have a few calls to make on the Hill this afternoon and then I'm going to drop in on Jeremy before I head home. I might be half an hour late."

Rory waved and Lisa was gone.

Rick noticed that something in Lisa's departure had really caught Billy Cleveland's attention. He had craned his neck to see her get into her car and drive away and then turned to Monica.

"Who's this 'Jeremy'?"

Monica shrugged. Zora said that Jeremy was just one of Lisa's clients.

When coffee hour was over, Rick retrieved Bronwyn and loaded her into her car seat, to her loud protests. Zora was off to a mink farm up the road in Greenland.

Billy and Monica drove off in a newish Jeep, quite a change from Monica's 15-year-old VW.

Rick waved all of them off and headed up the opposite hill.

The next day, Monica had a four-hour lunchtime

shift at the café. Billy had proposed that he drop her off and pick her up at the end, and use the time in between to look around the countryside.

He drove up through the reserve, then to Morgan-ville, out to Sissiboo Road and back to town. He ate lunch at the café and then wandered over to the Le-gion to have a beer and wait for Monica's shift to end.

The bartender and two patrons were in the mood for conversation. When they found out he came from away, they began to tell him everything they thought he should know about life in Bear River. The inform-ation flew thick and fast, but none of it was of much interest to Billy.

Finally, one of the locals asked, "How did you find your way to this little village?"

"I saw a TV news clip about the county fair here, with all the horses and oxen and stuff. There was a sharp-shooting show too. It seemed like the kind of place I might like to visit.

"Oh, yes, the Ex," the bartender said. "The Digby County Exhibition. Happens around the end of Au-gust every year. Its been going on for over 100 years. It sure was different this year, though!"

The bartender and the locals had a lot to say about the recent Exhibition. Was the new format better than the old one? Was it a good idea to mix it in with the Pow Wow? Was the food better or worse? There were divergent views among the trio, and little agreement.

The one point on which they agreed was that the

shooting show had been the highlight.

"The shooter looked pretty good on the TV news," Billy said. "Who was he, someone from around here?"

The bartender seemed to know the most. "They call him Jeremy Franklin. Lives out in Morganville, right across from that lady Marie who does mechanic work out there. He showed up about five years ago."

"He's kind of strange," one of the patrons said. "Kind of not like everyone else. He keeps pretty much to himself; hardly ever see him in town."

The other patron chimed in, "You can't miss Marie's place. There's a big fire truck in her yard now, waiting to be fixed. She's kind of odd too, but, man, can she fix cars and trucks!"

It was not hard to find the small house hidden in the trees across from the fire truck on Morganville Road. Billy drove in the driveway and parked behind an old car that looked like it had not been used for a while.

The front door of the house looked unused, so Billy went to the back door and knocked. There was no answer. He tried the door and found it was not locked so he opened it and in a raised voice said, "Is any body home? Julian?"

Again, there was no answer. He tried once more, stepping part way into the entryway this time.

A voice behind him said, "Julian's not here."

Billy turned. There was no one immediately behind him, but as he stepped out of the door, he saw a

30-year-old version of his brother Julian standing between two spruce trees at the edge of the forest that came nearly to the back door.

"Julian!" Billy exclaimed.

"Julian's not here," Jeremy repeated with no expression.

"Hey, I'm your brother Billy."

"No brother," Jeremy said, and he walked past Billy into the house.

Billy waited a moment to regain his composure, and then followed Jeremy in. He hung his coat in the entryway on the coat rack and found his brother in the kitchen giving a small cat a piece of fish from the refrigerator.

"Julian," he said, "we've been out of touch for years and years. It has taken me forever to find you. Where have you been hiding?"

Jeremy did not reply. He looked away, never at Billy, touched the cat more mechanically than smoothly, and stood without moving, as if in a half-stupor.

Billy tried again. "You must remember me, Julian, your big brother Billy. We lived together for a whole year in Fergus, remember, the year before you went away. You were 14 that year, just turned 15 before you left."

Jeremy stood silent for a long time, then murmured, seemingly to himself, "Fergus." He stood still for another long pause, then said, "Julian's not here."

He walked stiffly out the back door and out of sight. By the time Billy had followed him to the door himself, Julian had disappeared and did not respond to any further calls.

Billy went back inside to have a look around. He thought maybe he could find a bank statement or some other documents or clues helpful to his task.

As he was rummaging in an unused desk, a small pickup truck pulled in the driveway behind his car. An angry child's bellow emerged from the truck as the man he recognized from the coffee club as Rick the farmer opened the driver's door, got out and headed for the back entrance.

As he came in the door he called, "Hey, Jerry, are you home?"

In the kitchen, he stopped short at the sight of Billy Cleveland, Monica's new boyfriend.

"Hello Rick," Billy said, with a welcoming smile. "Monica said Ju…Jeremy likes visitors but doesn't get many, so I thought I would come out and introduce myself. He just left a minute ago, said he had to do something in the woods. You know what he's like."

"Zora asked me to bring Jerry some pills for his cat. She said just to leave them in his coat pocket if he wasn't home, so that's what I'll do. No point bringing Bronwyn inside if Jerry's not here."

Rick had a small paper bag in his hand. He turned and went back into the entry way where he fumbled to get the bag into a coat pocket. As he did so, his hand encountered a bit of stiff paper or something in the very depth of the pocket where he intended to lodge the paper bag. Reflexively he pulled it out and was surprised to find a business card, somewhat

tattered as if lost in the pocket for a long time: 'William Ferrante, Consultant...'

Then he realized he was putting the pills in the
wrong coat. There were two coats hanging on Mel
Prime's whale-tail coat rack; this one must be Billy's.

He switched to the other coat which was Jeremy's
own. He popped the bag of pills into a pocket, gave
Rosie, who had come to check on him, a good long
pat, and was back in the truck and out the driveway
with Bronwyn in full vocal complaint.

Billy waited a few minutes and then drove away.

11: Late nights

Zora had done all the baby duty that night: nurse, bath, play, nurse, play, change and slowly off to sleep after an hour of rocking in the baby carrier. Zora also had appointments starting at 8:30 the next morning, so Rick was back on duty when Bronwyn called for attention at 3 am. This was just part of being a dad as far as Rick was concerned, but it required some practice to accept that the middle of the night was a time to be up and doing, like any other night shift work, he supposed.

Sharing enough sleeping time with Bronwyn to add up to six or seven hours in a day required more in the way of acquired skills and creativity, and also some resistance to social convention: "You missed our lunch meeting because you were sleeping?!"

On this particular middle-of-the-night call to action, Bronwyn was business-like and efficient in her quests for food and a clean diaper, but she was doing poorly at getting back to sleep. Rick had walked her gently through the house in the baby sling with Erik Satie filling the air, but Bronwyn could not get her eyes to close.

At times like this, Rick was glad he was part of the

computer age. With Bronwyn strapped to him, he could put his laptop on a high table and type and mouse with both hands while continuing to rock her.

Tonight, as he gazed at the screen, he found his tired mind wandering back to that old business card he had found in what he supposed was Billy Cleveland's coat pocket. It was that family name on the card, Ferrante, that had stuck with him. That name had come up in conversation recently, but where and when and how he could not bring to mind. He knew there was a widely-read Italian author by that name, but she was not the connection he was looking for.

To pass the time and avoid any hard thinking, he tried searching the web for 'Ferrante', and then for 'William Ferrante'.

There was one hit high up on the first screen of the search results. A newspaper, the *Waterloo Region Record*, had reported just a few weeks ago that a strong explosion had destroyed a house in the nearby town of Fergus, Ontario. The owner of the house was facing delays in his insurance claims because the police considered the cause of the explosion suspicious.

The article mentioned a William Ferrante as a previous tenant of the destroyed home. He had departed some days prior to the explosion.

The next several screens of search results were not of interest, but as he scrolled further, there were three more articles involving a Julian Ferrante, all from the *Guelph Mercury* newspaper. The first two were from two days apart in 2004. One reported that a Julian Ferrante, aged 15 years, had died suddenly at the home he shared with his elder brother in Fergus, cause of death undetermined, grieved for by his father, George, stepmother, Roselyn and brother, William. The second reported that the body of the deceased Julian Ferrante had disappeared from the crematorium less than an hour before the cremation itself was to take place.

The third was from 2002, about a shooting club in Fergus that had just won a provincial tournament. The big win had been due to the extraordinary marksmanship of a 13-year-old club member from Toronto named Julian Ferrante, who just never missed his target. Julian was being groomed to join Canada's Olympic team in a few years' time, when he would be old enough. His Father, George, and mother, Roselyn, were very proud.

Wait! Julian Ferrante! That was the name he had been searching for in his head. Marie had used it a month ago, when she was talking about how Jeremy came to be living near her. That used to be Jeremy's name; Jeremy was Julian is Jeremy, the sharpshooter extraordinaire.

Stepmother Rose and Marie had changed his name and brought him to Morganville to protect him from, from what? From his older brother, Marie had said, and this Julian Ferrante had had a father, George, and a stepmother, Rose.

And Rick had noticed the business card of one William Ferrante in Billy Cleveland's old coat pocket this afternoon. *What the hell is this all about?*

There were two more hits for "William Ferrante." A newspaper archive from the Dalhousie University library offered something from 1999 in the *Annapolis County Spectator*. It described two nearly-fatal cases of shellfish poisoning in which the victims, a William Ferrante and his travelling companion, were saved by fast medical intervention at the hospital in Bridgetown. William's father, George, had made a large financial contribution to the hospital in gratitude.

The other search hit made no sense to Rick at first. It was a report in the *Winnipeg Free Press* from 2001 about a police raid on a local motorcycle gang called C-Company. Only when he scrolled down to the very end did he see the name William Ferrante highlighted. It was in a list of the people rounded up in that raid but subsequently released without charge.

On a whim, he tried a search on "Billy/William Cleveland". After many screens of personal Facebook pages, he found only one faintly-interesting hit. Some kind of gangland street fight in Vancouver in 2014 had left a street person named Billy Cleveland, age 33, dead on the sidewalk. No kin, no funeral, no grieving.

Finally, Bronwyn had fallen asleep. Rick gingerly moved her from baby sling to crib. She took a few alarming fast, anxious breaths and flailed the air with her arms and legs, but then relaxed, gave one little kick, and was asleep again.

Rick saved the search results so he could verify in

the morning that he had not just dreamt it all, and snuck into bed.

Bronwyn slept in until 9 the next morning and so did Rick. He could hardly believe the clock when she at last gave the wakeup call.

After a good breakfast, she started making an odd sound, blowing bubbling noises out between her lips in repeated short bursts: *bhhhft bhhhft bhhhft bhhhft*. She looked expectantly at Rick as she did this, as if she were making a request he was supposed to understand.

He didn't get it, but Bronwyn seemed game for something, so he bundled her up and took her down to the milking barn to check in with Jérôme Weaver, the milk boss.

The last of the cows were moving through the parlour for the morning milking when they arrived. As they waited for Jérôme to finish up, Mathilde, the long-serving matriarch of the herd, spotted them at the fence and began stalking toward them, her head held low, her eyes fixed on them, her massive horns extending nearly three feet straight out on each side of her big hairy head like the woolly mammoth version of a Texas Longhorn.

Rick sat Bronwyn on the top rail, and she squirmed with anticipation as Mathilde slowly came up to them. Mathilde raised her head, her eyes crossed and the whites bulging as she focused her vision at the end of her own nose and placed it half an inch from Bronwyn's eager neck.

Fhhht fhhht fhhht, fhhht.

There it was! Bronwyn's morning sound, the quiet rapid sniffs from Mathilde's nostrils held right against Bronnie's ear. Would these go down in history as Bronwyn's first words?

The tip of Mathilde's tongue slowly extended from under her nose and she gave Bronwyn's neck a single soft caress. Bronwyn wriggled and giggled. Mathilde gave Bronwyn one last sniff, then lowered her head, anticipating the good scratch around the ears that Rick proceeded to give her.

Bronwyn had become a centre of Mathilde's attention from their very first encounter when Bronwyn was one week old. If Mathilde saw Bronwyn even from a half mile away, she would make a beeline for her and try to inspect her as closely as she could, as if judging Rick and Zora's parenting skills against her own standards, gleaned from the experience of having had 12 calves during her 14 years.

Mathilde had been Uncle Gilles's favourite and Jérôme Weaver had been Uncle Gilles's best friend. Mathilde was never going to find herself on the beef side of Lansdowne Highland's business.

Jérôme finally came over to them, his gait slightly uneven. Jérôme had gotten his name from the famous castaway found on the beach at Sandy Cove in the 1860s. His relatives of many generations ago had helped care for the original Jérôme, and his family still felt a kinship with that story.

The original Jérôme was a youngish man whose legs had been surgically amputated. The name had been prophetic for Jérôme Weaver; as a young man he had lost a leg in an accident on a fishing trawler, and now got around on an artificial one.

He scratched Mathilde, and tickled Bronwyn, too. "You're stuck with it now, Rick," he said. "That new cheese is going out into the world as 'Highland Bronnie's Triple Scream'. The labels just came back from the printer."

They chatted about farm business for a while; then Rick and Bronwyn headed back to the house.

It was time for mid-morning milk for Bronwyn and coffee for Rick, but recently Bronwyn had started insisting on some bread and a crumb or two of cheese, too. The diapers were getting worse and the morning nap sounder and longer, and maybe at some point she would need a lot less from Zora; it all seemed a fair trade-off.

During her late-morning nap, Bronwyn could sleep through almost any noises, so Rick made good use of this time to vacuum the whole place, motivated into extra thoroughness by the fact that his mother-in-law was coming late in the afternoon and staying the night. Rick got on well with Lilian Cromwell, but Lilian was a high-school principal, used to setting and keeping high standards.

As he dusted, moved furniture, sucked up the week's accumulated debris and cleaned the two bathrooms, Rick found himself confused and worried about this William Ferrante person he'd found on the Internet, about Monica Jeffries's new boyfriend, Billy Cleveland, and about what it all might mean for his friend Jeremy. He decided he would talk to Marie about it as a first step.

But right now, it was Bronnie wake-up time and their team lunch time, and they already had a full afternoon ahead of them.

Lilian arrived at 5:30 and had shooed Rick and Zora out the door by 6:00. Lilian insisted that Rick and Zora should have "date nights" as often as possible, with no Bronwyn and no work calls, and she came herself one weekend each month to make sure this happened at least that often.

This time, Rick and Zora were headed for a new restaurant in Annapolis Royal that featured food in the traditions of Spain. The restaurant's seafood paella already had become locally famous, and Rick and Zora were keen to try it.

It was worth the drive. The paella was chock full of lobster and scallops and squid and clams, and not a scrap of fish, seasoned so expertly that all potential clashes among the ingredients had been brought into perfect harmony.

They had requested a table for two in a quiet corner so they could talk without being concerned about who might overhear them. Zora told Rick her vet stories and he told her his farm and house-dad stories, including his virtual encounter with William Ferrante. They leaned in close to each other, laughed and laughed, and lingered over dessert so their wine could wear off and their heads clear before the drive home.

When they got into their truck, Zora pulled out

the breast pump and worked at producing Bronwyn's next lunch during the half hour drive home. Rick sometimes wondered how she kept this up, day after day, week after week, finding the time to be a nursing mother even while working away from home all day long. Just the thought of it wore him down and he wished he could do more to relieve Zora of this endless duty.

When they arrived home, Lilian and Bronwyn were sound asleep. Zora put her collected milk in the refrigerator and turned to Rick with the radiant smile and flashing eyes that had knocked him right off his feet five years ago.

"The rest is all for you Ricky," she said, and enveloped him in the deepest and longest full-body kiss the universe thus far had ever witnessed. Then she grabbed his hand and yanked him away to the bedroom.

12: Where are you?

Lisa Willson stopped her car on the Morganville Road, at the turn onto the south end of Parker Road. She was headed for Bonnie Cheever, her next client. It was 3 pm on a Tuesday afternoon. She called Bonnie and told her she would be at her door in a few minutes. Bonnie could just stay in her bed if she preferred and not worry about who was walking into her house.

Lisa loved her work as a home-service nurse. She liked meeting and caring for people where they lived, helping them remain at home where they felt most secure while providing them with the medical care they needed. She never thought of her job as working alone because she was always with her patient, and often with the patient's whole family.

Like Zora, who often vaccinated dogs and cats as a complementary service on her farm calls, Lisa often provided medical care beyond the immediate purpose of her visit to families who otherwise likely would just have done without.

Bonnie lived on the old Cheever homestead on the river side of Parker Road. It seemed a lonely place, with no close neighbours and the road impassable at various times of year due to mud or ice or snow.

On the whole, Bonnie was a spry and healthy 85-year-old, but she had fallen down the stairs and sprained an ankle recently and she needed both pain medication and encouragement to get herself up and moving around again. She lived alone, with various members of her large clan bringing her whatever she needed from time to time.

Lisa tried to visit her once a month, just to keep an eye on her health.

She parked her car beside the old barn and found Bonnie in her bedroom on the ground floor of the house, having been roused from her afternoon nap by Lisa's call. Lisa watched Bonnie walk with her crutches, gave her a few pointers and some pills for pain, and re-wrapped her ankle in a new elastic bandage for maximum support.

Bonnie insisted that Lisa stay for a cup of tea, which Bonnie herself made with ease.

"My granddaughter, Millie, and her mom Becky are coming over tomorrow morning," she said. "We'll make cakes all day for the Fire Hall bake sale on the weekend."

Lisa concluded that Bonnie was doing just fine. She checked out Bonnie's current collection of medications, confiscating the many out-dated and contraindicated pills that family and visitors regularly brought to her from their hordes of uncompleted prescriptions. A senior's multivitamin and some naproxen were all she left behind.

This was Lisa's last call of the day, and she headed

out to her car with a light step, buoyed up by the thought of surprising Rory by arriving home early. This time, she could fix supper for him for a change.

As she was extracting her keys from her handbag, an iron hand was clapped across her face and one of her arms was forced up behind her back so hard that she felt her shoulder tendons tear.

"Ah, my little nursey, it's about time you and me got together." It was Rex Cheever.

Rex dragged Lisa through a half-open doorway on the side of the barn away from the house, his hand all but preventing her from breathing. He threw Lisa to the floor and shifted his grip to her throat.

"There's no one gonna hear you now," he said. "Mama's deaf as a snake. But you won't do much yelling anyway if you know what's good for you."

He let go of her throat, hit her a knock-out blow in the face with his fist, and grabbed her by the throat again, tightening his grip as he began tearing off her clothes with his free hand.

"You won't tell no one, neither," he hissed, breathing hard. "You tell someone and that little fairy husband of yours will get his kneecaps torn off."

He paused to rip off her bra.

"You're gonna like me a lot, compared to that little faggot."

Lisa could feel herself cut and torn as Rex ripped away her remaining clothing. As he became more excited, his grip on her throat became tighter and tighter until finally she could not breathe at all; she struggled violently for a moment and passed out.

She came to on a hard wooden floor in the dark, hurting everywhere, terrified and trying to understand where she was and what had happened. In the darkness, she could see a thin line of light on the floor about 20 feet away.

She could not raise one of her arms, but managed to crawl to the light and kick at it. A door swung open and daylight poured in.

She stumbled to her feet. She was bleeding in many places. Her clothes were in tatters and strewn on the floor. She found enough of her blouse and pants to partially cover herself.

She wanted to run away as fast as possible, but she thought that her ripped-up clothing might be needed as evidence by the police. She gathered up what she could find.

She found her handbag and keys on the ground where she had dropped them. She eased herself painfully into her car and drove away up Parker Road.

~

Marie had told Rick that she would be home after about 2 pm, if he wanted to come over and talk about whatever it was that was on his mind. She had finished the fuel injector job on the fire truck's ancient diesel engine that morning and had driven it to the village to test her work and to deliver it back to the fire hall. She had decided to celebrate the lovely fall day by walking back home up the river road, an hour or so of good exercise along the moss-banked barley-water brook under bright yellowing leaves.

Rick and a howling Bronwyn arrived shortly after she had reached home herself. Marie took Bronwyn for a little walk around the yard to let her recover from the perceived indignities of the drive over, and then they went inside.

Rick described to Marie his encounter with Billy Cleveland at Jeremy's house two days before, and of finding the business card of William Ferrante in Cleveland's coat pocket. He had brought along print-outs of the items he had found online.

Marie became increasingly agitated as Rick's story unfolded. She had never met any of these Ferrantes, only Rose. She wouldn't know William Ferrante if she saw him, but Rose had taken extreme steps to make sure Jeremy's brother would never find him.

"Jeremy has been acting very strangely the last two days," she said. "He was hiding in the forest when I called on him yesterday. He seemed fearful of everything. I don't think he had eaten anything all day, so I made him come to my place for a meal. He was silent and awkward, much like he was when he first arrived here."

Rick said, "Why don't Bronwyn and I go across the road and see if we can entice Jeremy back here for coffee. Maybe you and I can get him to talk a little about his visit from Billy Cleveland."

"It's worth a try."

While Rick and Bronwyn went to find Jeremy, Marie called Thomas French in Toronto, to ask if he had learned anything lately about William Ferrante. Mr. French said he had not and that he did not expect William ever to contact him again.

The only news he had had recently was that the house William had been renting in Fergus Ontario had been blown to smithereens a few weeks ago. It had happened so expertly that the police suspected criminal activity, and there were rumours that traces of gelignite had been found in the wreckage, according to Mr. French's friends in insurance. William had cancelled his lease and moved out two days before the explosion. Mr. French had no idea where William might have gone.

As Rick and Bronwyn came up to Jeremy's back door, Rick shouted, "Jerry, it's Rick and Bronnie. Are you home?"

He entered the kitchen and was about to call again when Jeremy came in through the back door behind him. Bronwyn wriggled happily.

Jeremy walked stiffly up to Rick, took Bronwyn and enveloped her completely in his arms. He stood there a long while with Bronwyn, immobile as a post, like a still photo of a soldier returning to his family from war.

"Marie is making coffee for us, Jerry," Rick said. "Bring Bronnie and let's go over."

He pulled Jeremy's coat from the rack in the entry way, draped it over Jeremy's shoulders, and they walked back across the road to Marie's.

~

It was that special ring tone Rory had programmed his phone to make when the caller was Lisa, the one ring that never could happen too often.

He stopped writing mid-sentence and answered. "Hi sweetheart!"

A harsh voice he could hardly recognize as hers began speaking. "He raped me, Rory; he tried to kill me. He broke my shoulder." Tears and pain choked her words.

Rory's heart nearly stopped. "Who? Lisa, where are you?"

"At the top of Parker Road. I can hardly talk. He strangled me."

"I'm coming right now. I'll borrow a car. I'll be there very soon."

Rory was not quite controlling his panic but tried to think clearly. Lisa shouldn't stay alone for the half hour it would take him to find a car and get to her. "Lisa, can you drive a little further, to Marie's, and wait there?"

"I think I can. I'd rather wait there. I can; I'll go there now."

It was a 10-minute fast run from their house to the café. Rory told Greg, the owner, that Lisa had had an accident out on her rounds and needed him urgently. Greg handed him the keys to the Café's van and Rory was off.

Rick and Marie sat at Marie's kitchen table, sipping her good coffee and making small talk in the hope that Jeremy might move closer to them and join in, in his own way. Jeremy had put his coffee cup on the windowsill in the next room and was wandering around near it, holding the now sleeping Bronwyn close to him.

The sound of tires rolling over the gravel in her driveway caught Marie's attention and she went to the kitchen door to see who had just driven in. Her face went white.

"My God!" she exclaimed and raced out the door.

Rick got to the door in time to see Marie helping Lisa out of her car. Lisa was half naked. She was bleeding from face and arms and shoulders, her left eye was bloodshot, her left cheek a huge swollen purple bruise. She was clinging to Marie with her right arm while her left arm dangled oddly straight down.

Rick raced down the steps to help and together they got Lisa up to the deck and into the kitchen. Lisa was crying and coughing and still gasping hoarsely for breath as they helped her onto a kitchen chair.

"He raped me, Marie. Rex Cheever. I was leaving Bonnie's. He choked me and dragged me into the barn. He strangled me; I think I almost died. I must have passed out. I was alone in the barn next thing I knew. He said he would destroy Rory if I ever told anyone."

Marie fetched a house coat and wrapped it around Lisa, removing as she did so the ripped-up remnants of her clothing. She pulled a bottle of Armagnac from a cupboard and poured a wine-glass full for Lisa and more modest portions for herself and for Rick.

"Rory's coming here," Lisa said. "He just had to borrow a car."

As she spoke, there was a rattle of stones in the road and tire noise up the driveway. A moment later, Rory came bursting through the kitchen door. When he saw Lisa, his face contorted in horror and he ran to her, hugging, sobbing, asking, gently touching her wounds.

Marie poured another wine-glass full of Armagnac, set it beside Lisa's, took Rick by the arm and moved with him into the living room where Jeremy was standing, watching. "Lisa has been badly hurt, Jerry," she said.

Jeremy stood transfixed by the scene in front of him. After a moment, he handed Bronwyn to Rick and walked slowly over to Lisa and Rory in the kitchen.

He bent over Lisa and studied her in silence, her face, her arms, her hands, her still-bloody hair. He reached out with one hand and gently touched the swollen bruise on her face.

Lisa took his hand and held it softly against her wounded cheek. "It's okay, Jerry," she said. "I'll be all better soon. Don't worry about me."

As he continued to study her wounded cheek, Lisa saw tears flowing down his own.

Jeremy withdrew his hand and stood up stiffly again. He turned to Rory and studied his face, too, for a moment, briefly holding eye contact. Then he picked up his coat and walked out the door.

As the Armagnac began to take effect, it dulled the horror of the moment enough for everyone's thoughts to move from agony and anger to action.

Lisa and Rory were not willing to let a fear of the Cheever clan keep them from reporting the rape and the rapist. Marie was afraid of the hardship and mental anguish a trial, or several trials, would place on Lisa in a legal system so biased against rape victims.

But Lisa needed to go to a hospital right away, whether or not she chose to report the assault to the police.

The Armagnac helped Lisa set aside her pain and humiliation and think of herself as a medical patient. She thought her left shoulder might be luxated and was worried that her vagina might be torn, with possibly serious consequences if not treated quickly. She also wanted a full forensic post-rape medical examination to collect legal evidence. For a forensic assessment, she knew that the hospital in Yarmouth was the nearest option.

"I don't need an ambulance to get to Yarmouth," she said. "I don't want all that public drama."

Lisa knew the rape kit nurse in Yarmouth from training sessions they had attended together. She phoned her to say she would be at the Yarmouth hospital in about an hour and wanted a rape kit exam.

"Lisa, have you been raped?" the nurse exclaimed in disbelief.

"Yes, a few hours ago."

"I'll stay here until we get you a full forensic," the nurse said. "Even if I have to be here all night." "We'll go in my car," Marie said firmly. "You can lie on the wide back seat."

She turned to Rory. "Take the van back to the café and we'll pick you up there."

Bronwyn was still asleep. Rick said, "Bronnie and I will go spend some time with Jeremy at his house. I'll make sure he eats a proper supper. If he wants, he can spend the night with us at the farm."

Rory zoomed off.

Rick helped Marie get Lisa comfortable in her car and off they went also. Rick and Bronwyn crossed the road to Jeremy's.

Jeremy was not in his house, so Rick went back outside to call him. As he did so, he noticed that Jeremy's coat was not on its usual whale-tail hanger in the entryway.

He and Bronwyn waited in the house for two hours, playing with Rosie, having a bath together in Jeremy's big bathtub and walking some short forest trails in the woods behind the house. He phoned Zora to explain and she said she would fix a supper that they could eat whenever he and Bronwyn got home.

As twilight gave way to darkness, Rick had to conclude that he was not going to see Jeremy again that evening. Jeremy was gone.

13: An angel came down

Henry Albert Pattinson Smith, Sheriff of Digby County at the turn of the 20th century, was not only a crack shot but also a conservationist in the mould of Teddy Roosevelt; he wanted lots of animals to shoot. Digby County was running low on native moose and caribou, so he helped organize the importation and release of some white-tailed deer, a creature new to the province.

The deer population rose slowly at first, then very quickly exceeded the capacity of the land to feed it and finally crashed to more sustainable numbers over the following one hundred years, during which time a local tradition of legal and illegal deer hunting became firmly established. As fall deepened and deer fattened, shots would ring out and bullets sail through the air, day and night.

So, when a shot rang out in the dark that Tuesday night, the only surprise was that the bullet managed to find its way through Rex Cheever's neck.

Constable Roger Laliberty's home telephone rang at 7 o'clock on Wednesday morning. Gerald Cheever, Rex's brother, told him that he had found Rex dead in his house. He asked Roger to come right away and take over all the official stuff that would have to be done. Gerald told Roger that he had visited Rex almost every morning and evening, to keep track of him for the family. This morning, he had found Rex dead in the living room, sitting in his chair in front of the TV.

Gerald sounded understandably shaken; Roger hurried over.

Rex's body was seated in his armchair but the part above his mid-torso sprawled over the chair's left arm. His head was almost severed at the neck. What must have been all the blood in his body had gushed onto the chair and floor, leaving coagulated pools.

It was an awful scene; Roger wished Gerald could have been spared seeing it. He took a brief statement from Gerald about when he had last seen Rex alive and when he had found him dead, and then urged Gerald to go and do whatever he felt he should do to let his family know.

Roger called the Digby RCMP station to report that Rex Cheever was dead and appeared to have been murdered in his own living-room. The Staff Sergeant told him to secure the scene and remain in place until a homicide team from Halifax could get there, maybe by mid-afternoon.

Roger erected a barrier of yellow crime scene tape around the house and driveway. He took photos of the living room from all angles with his phone's camera and then began his own technical inspection of the scene.

The television was still on, so Roger assumed Rex

must have been watching TV, or sleeping in front of it. Since Gerald had visited Rex the previous evening, the murder must have taken place sometime afterwards.

The white wall about six feet to the left of the chair was heavily spattered with blood around an imploded hole three or four inches in diameter. Based on the massive wound and the hole in the wall, Roger guessed that the murder had been carried out with a shotgun at close range, by someone in the room and close to Rex.

He tried to get a view along the line of fire from the hole in the wall and across the chair to estimate where the murderer might have stood. As he did so, he found himself looking across the room at the right-hand side of a large picture window that was framed by smaller side windows that could be opened for ventilation. The small side window on the right was open 6 or 7 inches.

The picture window looked out across a small field to the edge of the forest about 150 feet away. Someone hidden at the forest edge could easily have watched Rex through the big window and chosen his or her moment to attack.

Roger was tempted to start looking harder for evidence, which he knew would anger the homicide team, so he decided he had better wait outside. He strolled out in front of the picture window, looking through it as he imagined the murderer could have done. The view would have been very clear with lights on in the room and darkness outside. He backed away to the edge of the field, and even at that distance a voyeur easily could have tracked Rex's movements inside the house.

As he moved along the field edge examining the view of the living room, his foot came down on a small hard object, a rifle shell, tarnished grey-brown with age.

He picked it up: .30-30 was inscribed on the base, a calibre that was once a favourite locally for deer hunting. The grey-brown patina of tarnish covering the outer casing had a few thin scratches through it. The interior smelled faintly of burned gunpowder.

There was a squeal of tires and flashing lights in the road, and a van and two patrol cars pulled up in front of the house. The homicide team had arrived quickly! Roger put the shell in his jacket pocket and hurried over to the new arrivals.

Sergeant Harper was the senior investigator, a man Roger knew and respected. Roger briefed the team on what limited observations he had made thus far in the house, and the team began its work.

Harper said, "Have a senior family member come and make a formal identification of the victim and authorize a forensic autopsy."

"Yes, sir.."

"After that, I want you to interview all neighbours within a mile or so of the house. Maybe somebody heard or saw something."

Roger contacted Gerald again, and Gerald said he could come back to represent the family in about an hour.

Roger decided to use the waiting time to interview some neighbours. As luck would have it, Purley Jordan, the nearest neighbour, came driving along the road before Roger could even get in his car to go looking for him.

Purley rolled down his window. "How are you, Roger? Seems like you Mounties got some good news for us today."

He beamed and smiled as Roger solemnly confirmed that Rex Cheever was dead.

"Did you hear any shots last night or see anyone around?"

"Who wants to know?" Purley asked with a scowl. Then he winked. "I guess you ain't Lands and Forests, are you? I heard two rifle shots last night and I found a deer gut pile in my orchard this morning that wasn't there yesterday evening. They're probably frying up the liver for lunch right now. I seen nothing else, Roger. Don't you look too hard for the killer. This town would give them a medal. We'd crowd-fund them a vacation to Cuba if we know'd who they was. Now my girls can walk on the road again."

Purley laughed, waved and drove away.

When Gerald arrived to do the paperwork, Roger was surprised to see he had brought along his mother, Bonnie. He helped her out of the car, and she walked into Rex's house on her crutches.

Rex's body had not been touched or moved, and nobody had done anything to make the murder scene less ugly.

Bonnie stood a little away from the chair and stared at Rex for a long minute. Then she turned away and walked into the kitchen, where the papers to be signed were laid out on the table. The Sergeant gently explained what the paperwork was all about and where he hoped she would sign.

She took the offered pen and signed without hesitation. "That body is Rex, my son," she declared. "I bore seven strong children, but he came with nothing but evil in his heart. Now God's sent an angel down to take him back."

She turned to Sargent Harper. "Sir, you just do what you gotta do, but make no mistake, justice was served here last night. There ain't no more of it left to look for."

Two more RCMP vans arrived as Gerald and Bonnie were driving away. The corpse of Rex was loaded into one and driven off to the medical examiners in Halifax.

Three dogs and their handlers tumbled out of the other and prepared themselves for the chase.

~

Late on Tuesday night, a nurse wheeled Lisa out of the operating room, her vaginal tear stitched tight and her blood stream awash in antibiotics against the possibility of infection. Her luxated shoulder had snapped back into place with some expertly applied force and the orthopaedic surgeon thought it would stay there without further treatment.

Wednesday was a day of rest and of diminishing pain. Only Rory and her three close friends knew what had happened to her, they and Rex Cheever. Rory had not left her side. Marie had taken a room in a hotel nearby but had been with her all day.

Off and on, Lisa thought about what she should do next.

Late in the afternoon, there was a polite knock at her half-closed hospital room door, and Bonnie Cheever hobbled in.

"Bonnie!" Lisa exclaimed, astounded, "How did you ever find your way here?"

Bonnie gazed at Lisa for a long time, at her blue, swollen face, her black eye, her bandages. She sat gently on the edge of the bed, took Lisa's hand in her two hands, and began to cry.

"Rex done this to you Lisa. Somehow, he learned you was comin' that day. I should'a know'd; I should'a stopped it. I should'a shot him myself. I saw you drive away a long time after I thought you'd left, saw you come out of that barn all beat up. I come here to tell you it's my fault, Lisa. I bore him and I let him live and he done this to you."

Bonnie paused a moment to pull herself together and spoke again. "Gerald took me lookin' for you at your home, but weren't nobody there. The café told us you was here, said you'd had an accident. I asked Gerald to stay in the car. He don't know; don't nobody know."

Bonnie paused again. "Lisa, I come to tell you my son Rex can't hurt you no more. Rex was shot dead last night. God sent down an angel and took him back, is what I believe. You got to know this right away. You don't need to go through it all with the law now, tellin' it all again and again, feelin' it again every time. I done that once Lisa, long ago. Now you don't got to. Now you can feel safe in the village. You don't got to be scared or move away."

Lisa didn't know what to think or to say. Suddenly she was a rape victim with no rapist, her hand held by the once-rapist's mother seeking forgiveness for his crimes on the day he, her son, was murdered. Bonnie had come all the way to Yarmouth to liberate her from being a victim, to make as small as possible the scar Bonnie knew she was going to bear.

She reached around Bonnie with her good arm and pulled her into as close an embrace as she could manage. "Rex raped me, Bonnie. He hurt me. But Rex was sick. His mind was as sick as cancer. Don't you blame yourself for that. I'll be better soon. Rory will get me through this. We are not afraid in Bear River. It's people like you who keep us there. I'll be seeing you again next month, like I always do."

They cried quietly together for a while, then Bonnie stood up, looked at Lisa again, and headed for the door.

"Wait," Lisa said. "Bonnie, your ankle bandage is loose. Come sit on the bed again. Rory, just bring that chair over to put her leg up on. I'll show you and you can wrap it tight for her again."

14: We found nothing

On Wednesday morning, Bronwyn discovered bananas and Rick's life was transformed. One of the dairy men offered her a small piece from his breakfast, and it was love at first bite. Suddenly, a piece of banana was all it took to keep her content in her car seat. It was a liberation: no screams, no struggles, just a bit of sweet mush and some extra laundry because of the mess she made with it.

The discovery was well-timed because, this day, drive they must. They had driven to Morganville twice already to see if Jeremy was home, and now in the afternoon they had arrived for a third. visit. Again, he was not there. Rick noticed that Rosie's food bowl had been refilled since their last visit, and, since Marie was in Yarmouth, he surmised that Jeremy must have stopped by long enough to feed his cat.

As they drove away, Bronwyn fell asleep. It was her nap time, so Rick decided to cruise through Bear River and have some car window conversations until Bronwyn had her quota of sleep.

His first chat was with Purley Jordan by the post office. Purley was a-bubble with the news that Rex

Cheever had been killed in the night, shot in his house, best news ever. This was the first Rick had heard of it, but everyone else seemed in the know.

When Rick made a dash into the café to grab a takeout coffee, Rex Cheever seemed to be the only topic of conversation and the mood was upbeat. On a whim, he bought two cups and then drove up to Rex Cheever's house.

As he had anticipated, he found Roger Laliberty in the road, leaning against his patrol car, talking on the phone. Rick stopped beside Roger, rolled down his window and handed him the second cup of coffee. Roger's face lit up with appreciation. He turned away to finish his conversation and then turned back to Rick with a big smile, taking a sip.

"Busy day, Roger?"

Roger gave Rick a summary of all he had seen and done since that 7 am phone call. The homicide team had nearly finished its initial work, but Roger had been told that he would have to spend the night in the house to ensure the crime scene was not disturbed in any way. Some fingerprint and ballistics experts would be coming from Halifax tomorrow morning. They figured the projectile that went through Rex Cheever's neck likely was still in the wall, and they were going to cut out that piece of wall and bring it back to the crime lab.

"At the moment," he said, "everyone seems to think it was a shot gun at close range. The lab and the medical examiner will figure that all out, but it could take them quite a while."

As they talked, the tracker dogs and their handlers came back across the small field behind the house, and the handlers loaded the dogs into their van.

One of the handlers came over to Roger. "We found nothing. There was no scent of interest in or around the house. That big-eared bloodhound sniffed something at a spot along the field edge. We put the other two dogs on the same spot and all three started following something in a straight line southeast."

He added that the dogs took them over to the East Branch, way upstream from the power plant, but then they seemed to lose the trail, and that was that. They had brought the dogs across to the other side and gone up and down half a mile or so in each direction, but the dogs did not find anything more.

The dog van drove off and Roger turned back to Rick. "Cheever's neighbours aren't much interested in the police investigation."

He had questioned people at the six houses within a mile of Rex's house. Purley said he heard two shots in the night and found a gut pile in his orchard. Roger had verified the gut pile. Other neighbours said they had heard nothing and seen nothing, and that no dogs had barked. Several said that there were plenty of stray bullets flying around in the fall of the year, not too surprising someone would get hit by one sooner or later. So, the investigation had no leads.

"Once the ballistics guys dig out some bits of pro-

Ted Leighton

jectile with gun barrel marks on them, they'll probably be back to look for the weapon and take matters forward from there."

Roger figured the investigation would start slowly and take a long time. Once it really got underway, he wouldn't be able to talk about it anymore.

As their conversation was ending, Greg from the café drove up and pulled a picnic cooler out of his car. "A Sergeant Harper called the café and asked me to bring you a good supper," he said, handing the cooler to Roger. "He said you'd need breakfast in the morning too. We open at 6:30. What do you like for coffee in the morning?"

"I'll probably need a double shot in the dark by then," Roger said.

"You got it," Greg said, and drove off.

Bronwyn had slept too long already. Rick drove to the pump station on the flats, carried her over to the brook and helped her shake off sleep by dipping her feet in the cold water. This always made her squeal and laugh.

When they got home, Zora was in the kitchen, heating up one of Rick's casseroles and talking on the phone. Rick took Bronwyn upstairs and returned 15 minutes later with her changed and bathed. Zora took Bronwyn to feed and filled Rick in on her conversations with Marie and Lisa.

Lisa had told her about the surprise visit by Bonnie Cheever and said that she had decided not to report the rape to the police. She wanted everyone to think she had been in a car accident, slipped off a

122

back road into a boulder. The only people who would know otherwise were Rory, Marie, Jeremy, and she and Rick.

"Marie says Lisa is out of the woods medically and recovering fast. She also says no one will believe a story about a car accident without a damaged car to show for it. Lisa's and Rory's car is parked behind Marie's house and tomorrow, Marie is going to do some visible damage to the car and send it to the crusher. Lisa and Rory can use the car Marie likes to keep parked at Jeremy's until she builds them a replacement."

Rick laughed. It seemed like such wonderful rural life theatre, inspired by circumstances, practical, covering all the bases and beautiful in design. There was nothing to be gained, and maybe much to lose for Lisa, by blaming something new on the dead Rex Cheever. He hoped the murder investigation would not poke its nose into her accident.

It was 9 pm. Zora had to be on the Tiverton ferry at 6:30 tomorrow morning. She gave Rick a kiss, handed him Bronwyn, and went off to bed.

Bronwyn had slept too much and eaten too well, and looked to have 2-3 hours left in her before sleep. Rick bundled her up and took her out for a walk in the crisp, star-filled night. They walked the half mile to the far side of the pasture behind the house, accompanied there and back by Mathilde.

Tickle time, roll-over time, I'm-gonna-start-crawling-pretty-soon time, toy time, cat time, and it was time for that last, maybe, meal of the night. Rick figured that two finger-widths of cheap scotch might fairly be his due now too, so he and Bronwyn sipped their nightcaps together. Then he put her in the baby sling, facing heart to heart, and began her slow rock off to sleep.

It was indeed a slow rock tonight, no fuss but no closed eyes either. It was the kind of evening when he might get in an hour of screen time before Bronwyn was sufficiently out of it to go into her crib.

Rick was feeling philosophical about life and death after all the events of the past 24 hours, so he logged onto his favourite blog locator service on history and philosophy in science. Most of the items on offer were beyond what his tired mind was up for tonight, but one piqued his interest: "Lessons from Jérôme, the legless man from Meteghan."

It turned out to be a hyped-up title for a video of a lecture given way back in 1990 in a history of medicine series, on-line now because of some retrospective event within the historical society where it had been presented. The speaker was a psychiatrist, who said he was going to present the facts of Jérôme, such as they were, and then offer his own medical interpretation.

The dude was very formal but soft-spoken, and really seemed to have done his homework in the archives. He stuck to the facts and didn't speculate. "In the end," he said, "all we really know is that the man we have decided to call Jérôme was a young man working in the New Brunswick woods in 1860, when by misadventure of some kind his legs were frozen and had to be amputated below the knee."

Jérôme was universally noted to be demented or to behave oddly, with no social skills and no language. The New Brunswick county that had to look after him resented his material and nuisance costs to them, and hired a ship to drop him off across the Bay of Fundy in Nova Scotia to free them of both. There he became the ward, first of the province and then of the federal government, and lived with a few different families for forty-odd years until his death.

The psychiatrist dude said, "My only personal comment is that it seemed that everyone at the time assumed that Jérôme's mental conditions were the result of the personal trauma of his injury and amputation."

However, it seemed much more likely to the psychiatrist that Jérôme's mental illness was his primary disability, and that he actually had been marooned not once but twice: once when he must have been landed and abandoned in New Brunswick before his leg trauma, and again when he was dropped off on a Nova Scotia beach. The shrink proposed that Jérôme's abnormal mental condition was the main cause of these two abandonments and that the injuries he suffered were far more likely a consequence, rather than a cause, of his mental incompetence.

To Rick, it seemed the guy made a good case.

Bronwyn had lost interest in the video around the 1890 mark and had fallen asleep. It was midnight.

Rick poured Bronwyn into her bed as smoothly as he could and soft-toed it back down the stairs and into the kitchen, Jérôme and another finger or two of whisky on his mind. Young people with mental problems getting mistreated and hurt in various ways was no less an issue a hundred years ago than it was right now, it seemed. He refreshed his drink and turned to lean contemplatively against the kitchen counter. Only then did he notice Jeremy sitting at the kitchen table.

"Jerry!" he exclaimed. "I'm so glad to see you. Bronnie and I have been looking for you all day."

Jeremy looked like a woodsman at the end of a very long day. His boots and trouser legs were muddy and wet. The skin of his face, neck and hands was covered with a layer of fir needles and forest debris and a few smears of pitch. Unusual signs of fatigue and anxiety overlay his usual vacant expression.

Rick turned back to the counter, poured four fingers of whisky into another glass, and set it down in front of Jeremy. He took a chair across from him, held up his glass to Jeremy in half a toast and waited until Jeremy slowly moved his hand and picked up his own glass.

Rick tapped Jeremy's glass with his and said, "Here's to friendship."

Jeremy looked at the glass in his hand for a long time, then slowly half raised his glass, half lowered his head, and took a sip.

"Where have you been, Jerry?" Rick asked conversationally. "We went over to see you last night after Marie took Lisa and Rory to Yarmouth, but you'd already left.

"Woods," was Jeremy's only reply. He looked totally exhausted.

"Will you stay the night with us? Looks like you could use a good rest before you head off again."

Jeremy did not say no.

Rick told him to sneak upstairs and run a good hot bath (Jeremy didn't like showers) and to hand out his dirty clothes. He exchanged Jeremy's clothes for a pair of his own pyjamas and started a load of laundry.

When Jeremy emerged from the bathroom, Rick met him with Jeremy's mostly-unfinished whisky. "Knock this back Jerry," he said, "and then sleep until you can't sleep any more."

Somewhat to Rick's surprise, Jeremy downed the whisky in one go, evincing neither pain nor pleasure, handed Rick the empty glass, and went off to his bedroom.

15: Keenly interested

Rick awoke at 8 am, wondering how Bronwyn could have let him sleep so late. Zora was long gone, off to her monthly clinic in Freeport.

Rick made his way into Bronwyn's room to begin the day and froze in panic. Her crib was empty. His heart stopped. He was down the stairs in two jumps, wild-eyed and grasping for any explanation that was not unthinkable.

His panic ended just as abruptly. There she was on Jeremy's knee at the kitchen table, her diaper leaking abundantly onto his pyjama pants, making self-satisfied noises as she sampled bits of his bread and peanut butter.

Rick stood for a moment, shaking off the scenarios of kidnapping and murder that had passed through his mind during his two-second descent. With heart rate calmed and breathing resumed, he walked further into the kitchen.

"Good morning, Jerry," he said. "I owe you for a wonderful extra two hours of sleep and also for settling the question of when we should introduce Bronnie to peanuts."

He fired up the coffee pot, put Jeremy's washed

clothes out on the line, took Bronwyn up for a change and general cleaning, and returned with some clothes to lend Jeremy until his own were dry.

Jeremy never made coffee for himself, but he sometimes drank it when it was offered, and this morning he took a cup and nursed it like a professional.

Rick did the same while he also nursed Bronwyn. "Jerry, would you make me one of your peanut-butter-jam-toast-orange-juice, all-in-one-glass breakfasts? I've always wanted to try one."

Jeremy drained his coffee and went to work with determination, assembling the ingredients and making a three-slice version for each of them. Rick tried a spoonful and was pleasantly surprised. It was amazingly good, although Bronwyn was totally unimpressed.

They dug into their breakfasts until every last, wet crumb was consumed, then sat ruminating contentedly until Bronwyn became bored and called for action.

"Jerry," Rick said, "do you want to stay here with us for a while, or do you want to go home now?"

Jeremy was silent and stone-faced for a few minutes. Finally, he said, "Stay."

He was silent while Rick cleared up the table, then spoke again. "Rosie," he said.

"Let's go over and pick her up right now," Rick proposed. "She can stay here, too. She's done that before. Engelbert doesn't mind."

Engelbert, their testicle-free tomcat who nonetheless chased or copulated with any other cat that came his way, did neither to Rosie for some reason. Occasionally, they curled up together to sleep, but otherwise each did its own thing and they ignored each other.

Jeremy and Rosie moved in and stayed for a week. Jeremy liked being with the cows and the cows seemed to accept him as one of the herd. Mathilde pushed him around with her head when she felt the need, but never with her horns, and Jeremy seemed to understand her expectations and was obedient.

He went out with the herd to pasture and sometimes followed them into the milking line, much to the amusement of Jérôme Weaver. Jeremy would advance in single file with the cows until he reached a milking station, which he then just stepped through, or climbed down from to join Jérôme at the milking machines.

Jeremy seemed to delight in the smell of fresh silage and in watching the cows tear into the face of the silage pit when the electric fence that kept them from doing so most of the time was turned off for a while after milking. He liked doing the small jobs that Jérôme would propose to him from time to time.

He was not allowed in the cheese-making rooms, where craft and science and measurements and food safety where meticulously applied, but the cheese-makers gave him a daily supply of warm new curds, so fresh they squeaked in his mouth with every chew. Jeremy came as close as he ever did to smiling when eating those squeaky curds.

Most days, he just joined Rick and Bronwyn in their daily activities and the three of them ran the farm. Given the choice between running errands in Bear River or staying on the farm, Jeremy generally preferred the farm.

However, he did not miss much by avoiding the village that week. Despite being the scene of a gruesome murder, Bear River's heart had never skipped a beat. The fingerprint and ballistics teams were in and out in about six hours on the second day and the crime scene tape was removed. Three days later, the medical examiner released Rex Cheever's body to his family. It was buried in a small graveside ceremony attended by a few family members.

Roger Laliberty was back on his regular beat. He said to Rick, "I have no secrets to keep about the investigation because no new information has come my way."

Overall, the town seemed to share Purley Jordan's view of the matter: the less news the better.

On Friday night, Zora arrived home, followed closely by Melvin Prime. She had asked Mel to make some special horseshoes to help correct a lameness she was trying to fix, and when she picked them up, she invited him to come back to the farm for supper.

Friday night was pizza night, and Rick-the-chef was at the top of his game. He and Zora often made Friday night their movie night as well, and tonight Rick insisted that they all watch the psychiatrist dude's old lecture on the medical history of legless Jérôme before they watched the cliff-hanger.

At the end of the evening, Mel said, "Jeremy, I am itching to spend some quality time in the fall woods before winter sets in. Would you be up for a canoe trip?"

Jeremy looked away and nodded ascent, and so the deal was made.

"We'll go to Whitesand Lake," Mel said. "We can get there in a day from Sixth Lake, if there's not too much wind and you sit still. You're going to carry the big pack and the canoe, Jerry, on every carry! We'll use the Clarke cabin. We'll stay a week. We'll cut some firewood to pay our keep and we'll just watch the leaves turn red."

Early in the morning two days later, Rick and Bronwyn dropped off Mel, Jeremy and all their gear by the north shore of Sixth Lake.

"We'll be back here around four next Sunday afternoon to pick you up," Rick said.

As they drove away, he could see in the rear-view mirror Mel loading up Jeremy with the 80-pound pack and the canoe for the short walk to the lake.

Rick and Bronwyn had a big week ahead them, too. There was a lot of corn silage to get made. There was a lot of hay to truck in. The fourteen cows culled from the herd this fall had to be organized into sausage and ground beef. Bronwyn had some serious work to do pulling herself up against walls and furniture and practising her breast-stroke across the floor.

It was Thursday afternoon already before they even knew it.

The coffee club had missed two meetings, one because of Lisa's accident and a second to give her time to heal. Today they were back in full force. Marie had come also, because she had a project to propose to the club members.

Jeremy's birthday was the next week, on Wednesday. Jeremy himself couldn't have cared less, but Marie wanted to celebrate.

The coffee group included most of the people actually acquainted with Jeremy, they were clustered with Marie at one end of the table. Monica Jeffries joined this group, too, because Billy Cleveland was keenly interested in Jeremy, now that he had visited him once himself, and she was keenly interested in Billy.

"Jeremy doesn't like big groups," Marie said, "but he does seem to appreciate a fuss being made about him as long as he can watch it all from a distance."

She proposed that the group come to a party of cake and good cheer at her place in the late afternoon and then they would all go across the road to Jeremy's house for a potluck supper. They all would make a lot of extra food and freeze the leftovers at the end so that Jeremy could have these as good meals for himself well into the future. That food would be his birthday present, whether he saw it that way or not.

Marie said, "I'll make a seven-layer Icelandic cake with cardamom prune filling. I know Jerry likes that."

"Lansdowne Highland can make a special batch of

ice cream to go with the cake," Zora said. "What flavour?"

"Sex!" they chorused.

The following Wednesday afternoon, the party assembled as planned.

Mel and Jeremy had returned from Whitesand Lake the Sunday before, and Jeremy had gone back to his own house. Rick, Zora and Bronwyn came with ice cream and a big fish pie they knew was a favourite. Lisa and Rory came with quiches. Henry-the-songwriter knew Jeremy liked mince pies, so he brought 30 mince tarts, pre-packaged in pairs for freezing, and a big mince pie for the potluck itself.

Monica brought a big pan full of the famous seafood paella catered by the Spanish restaurant in Annapolis Royal. Billy had suggested this. Billy had to be away that evening and overnight, and couldn't join the party, but he had ordered the paella and had picked it up.

Monica had not been to Morganville before and she ended up, paella in hand, at Jeremy's house instead of Marie's.

"Can I just leave the paella here for later?" she asked.

He didn't say no, so she placed it on the kitchen counter and walked across the road to Marie's.

Marie knew how to throw a party. Arrivals quickly had glasses of good pink champagne in their hands, with endless refills in plain sight. Highland Bronnie's Triple Scream was on offer, along with with smoked mackerel and garlic-pickled chanterelles. It took about half an hour for everyone to arrive.

"Someone had better go get Jeremy before we start serving the cake and ice cream," Marie said.

"I'm on it," Zora called out, and she headed across the road to fetch the birthday boy.

When she arrived in Jeremy's kitchen, Rosie met her. Something about the cat caught her attention.

Rosie was walking in a really strange way and pawing oddly at her mouth. She seemed to be having trouble coordinating her hind legs. Her eyes were fixed in position, giving her a sort of startled zombie stare. She collapsed every few steps and was breathing heavily.

"Jerry?" Zora called out. There was no answer, but then Jeremy often did not answer people's calls.

Zora looked around the kitchen. A big aluminum container of food was on the counter, uncovered at one corner, with a serving spoon in it and a portion removed. The food looked like the paella from the Spanish place in Annapolis Royal she and Rick had liked so much. Zora guessed that Jeremy had decided to sample it ahead of schedule. A small bowl with a few rice grains in it was on the floor below the counter.

She walked further into the house, looking for Jeremy. She found him in the living room, seated on a chair. An empty bowl with a spoon in it was on the small table beside him. Jeremy did not move; his eyes were fixed, and his breathing was strange—an occasional deep breath with no breathing at all in between.

Lisa's phone beeped. As she dug it out of her bag to read the message, Rick's phone beeped too, the text-from-Zora beep.

"Come quick".

Rick looked up at Lisa. "Something's wrong," she blurted out and ran out the door. Rick handed Bronwyn to Marie with emergency in his eyes and ran after her.

They found Zora pawing frantically through some of the veterinary equipment in her truck parked in Marie's driveway. "They're dying", she said. "I think it's shellfish poisoning. Lisa, go see Jeremy; Ricky, call an ambulance."

She threw some items into her vet bag and ran back to Jeremy's house.

Lisa found Rosie laid out on the floor near where Jeremy sat. They both seemed to be gasping weakly for breath.

Lisa was trying to find Jeremy's pulse when Zora returned. "I watched a cat die from this a few months ago," she said. "Can you intubate Jeremy?" She had two tubes and two air bags of different sizes in her hand.

A look of deep anxiety came over Lisa's face. "I don't know how, Zora. It's not something I was ever taught to do."

Zora paused for five long seconds. "Here goes my career," she said, mostly to herself.

She pulled a small syringe and a bottle out of her bag, read the bottle's label quickly, glanced at Jeremy, sucked up a small volume from the bottle with the syringe needle, and handed the syringe to Lisa. "Diazepam, it's all I have. Give it to him quick, IV."

Lisa found a vein in Jeremy's arm and carefully injected the content into his blood stream.

Zora loaded another tiny syringe and injected a much smaller volume into Rosie's jugular vein. "Ricky, help us lay Jeremy out on the floor."

Rick and Lisa followed instructions, pulling Jeremy from his chair and laying him out flat and face up.

"God help me," Zora mumbled. "This size tube is meant for pigs. Ricky, shine that flashlight into Jerry's mouth."

She took the tube, smeared it lightly with lubricant, opened Jeremy's mouth with one hand and grasped his tongue, probed gently into the back of his throat with the tube and then, like a matador thrusting his sword, pushed the tube deep into Jeremy's windpipe.

She quickly inflated the little ring that would seal the tube in place, attached a bellows-like air bag to the protruding end of the tube, pumped the bag gently to ensure it was properly connected, and handed the bag to Lisa. "Breathe for him. Fill his chest gently and let the recoil push the air out again. Try every five seconds maybe; is that about the human breathing rate? I hope that ambulance has mechanical breathing equipment."

"It will," Lisa said. "They all do now."

She took over breathing for Jeremy at about the moment he stopped breathing for himself. "You're an angel, Zora."

Zora turned back to Rosie. "I'll remember you when I'm in jail," she said to the cat.

She grabbed the tiny tube and repeated her motions. "Breathe for her now, Ricky. A quarter cup of air is about what she needs, every three seconds or so. I'll spell you off."

She watched Lisa and Jeremy for ten or so breaths. She pressed a finger repeatedly into Jeremy's gums and watched the colour blanch and then slowly but reliably return.

"He's doing okay, I think," she said. "I'll do Rosie now, Ricky. You had better go tell the others what's happened."

Zora took over breathing for Rosie and Rick walked into the kitchen to go out the door.

"Jerry and Rosie ate some of that paella," Zora called after him. Rick glanced at the pan of food and hurried on to Marie's.

The party-goers already were coming down Marie's driveway, headed for Jeremy's to find out what was going on. As Rick began his explanation, the ambulance arrived with siren and flashing lights. Constable Roger Laliberty was right behind it in his patrol car.

"Jeremy has suffered some kind of sudden illness," Rick told the group. "Could everyone please go back to Marie's? I'll join you as soon as the ambulance leaves."

Marie handed Bronwyn to Rick. "If that ambulance is for Jerry, I'm going with him."

Marie, Rory, Rick and Bronwyn ran back to Jeremy's and the others withdrew to Marie's to await news.

The paramedics had rushed right in. "I think this man may have shellfish poisoning," Lisa told them.

The chief medic looked at Jeremy. "Who the hell intubated this guy?"

"I did," Lisa said. "I gave him some Valium first, IV."

The chief medic whistled in admiration. He gave Jeremy a quick examination.

"He'd be dead now without that tube," he said. "Let's get him to Yarmouth. They've got all the life support equipment."

They eased Jeremy onto a stretcher, put him in the ambulance and hooked him up to a mechanical respirator. The chief medic took charge and they were off. Lisa ran back inside.

Zora was on the floor, pushing air in and out of Rosie's lungs, tears of emotion and relief running down her face. "That was a very generous lie, Lisa."

"Zora, if Jerry survives, it will be because of you. You knew what was wrong and what to do. You're amazing."

"I see a lot of cats."

Rory asked, "How long will Rosie need help breathing?"

"It could be a few hours or a few days," Zora said.

"Can I help, maybe take a turn?"

She showed him how and Rory took over. "We had better find a board or something to lay Rosie on and take her back to my clinic," she said.

"You two can't keep this up for hours or days by yourselves." Rory said. "If I can do this, so can everyone else over at Marie's. They're not going to want to just drive away anytime soon. Why don't we all take turns with Rosie? It'll feel like we are doing something for Jerry, and we'll all be waiting together for news from Marie."

Well, why not? Zora thought. It would be like a wake in reverse, everyone on an all-night vigil trying to keep the man and his cat alive.

Rory and Lisa put Rosie on a cutting board and carried her carefully across the road to Marie's, breathing for her all the while, and Zora followed with Bronwyn. Roger and Rick were the only ones left behind

"What happened here?" Roger asked.

"Zora thinks Jeremy ate some bad shellfish and fed some to his cat. She saw a case in two cats a few months ago and recognized the signs. I guess we'll find out if she's right."

"Sounds all very medical," Roger said. "I think the RCMP can take its nose out of this one. I had better go report in and find out what's next for me tonight."

He went out to his patrol car and drove away.

Rick paused to study the pan of paella. *What if everyone had eaten some at the potluck instead of just Jeremy and the cat? What if other people were eating it now?*

He grabbed his phone and called the restaurant in Annapolis Royal to tell them what had happened.

The owner was horrified. He called out to his staff

to serve no more food, to retrieve everything already served, to apologize to the customers and to close the restaurant. He thanked Rick for calling, took his contact information and then said he had to ring off and call the public health hotline.

Rick resumed his inspection. The paella contained lobster, shrimp and squid in abundance, but no clams this time or anything like them. There was some fish, however.

That seemed odd to Rick, because the restaurant boasted that its seafood paella contained no plain old fish at all. This one had tiny white bits of fish mixed in everywhere. No teaspoonful would miss a piece.

The scientist in Rick kicked in: *better save some of the dish in case some kind of analysis would be needed later on.*

He took some photos of the paella pan as Zora had found it. Then he found some containers in a drawer and put the rice with fish bits in two of them and larger chunks of lobster, shrimp and squid in the others, all to take home and freeze.

What to do with the rest of the big pan of possibly poisonous food? There was a big burning barrel behind Jeremy's house and Rick decided incineration was the safest available means of disposal.

He got a fire going and threw in some dry hardwood. When it was burning good and hot, he layered in a mix of paella and wood until all the paella was in the fire. He tossed in the aluminum pan, too, and covered it all with another layer of wood.

It was a good burning barrel in a safe location. Rick decided he could leave the fire to burn on its own and ran over to join the others at Marie's.

16: Just enough

Billy Cleveland could have met the ambulance at the hospital in Yarmouth, had he known it was coming. But he had not anticipated such an ambulance. He had anticipated a night spent far away from his apartment in Annapolis Royal, possibly with another cute hotel night clerk, and a news report in the morning about a birthday party gone terribly wrong, with eight or ten people, 'Jeremy Franklin' among them, dead from food poisoning or as a cult suicide, whatever the media chose to believe.

He was sure Monica would faithfully have brought the paella to the potluck supper, and equally sure that she would not live to say any more about it. He would return as soon as the news was out, grieve appropriately and depart, broken-hearted, to try life again elsewhere. Soon, his lawyers would begin probing deeply into bank records and obscure legal precedents to find for him a pathway to Julian's trust funds.

While Billy was finishing his beer in a Yarmouth bar, Marie was in the ambulance watching the monitors that testified to Jeremy's continued existence, and Rick had rejoined the birthday party group still

143

gathered in Marie's house. Marie had just called to say that Jeremy was alive. His heart rate and blood pressure were very low but were stable and not yet life-threatening. Jeremy's hand in hers was still warm.

Max, the chief medic, had stated confidently that Jeremy would survive, but the only real evidence to support this was that he was not yet dead.

The news that Jeremy was holding on opened some space for other thoughts in Rick's troubled mind. He remembered that newspaper article he had found online about the Bridgetown hospital and saving William Ferrante's life after he and a travelling companion had gotten shellfish poisoning. Young William had told the reporter that, while he was paralyzed, all his senses had continued to work, that he could hear and understand and was terrified because the medics around him already considered him to be dead.

Rick shuddered at the thought and quickly called Marie to tell her that Jeremy might be able to hear and understand even though he couldn't move. "Keep talking to him, Marie. Let him know you know he's alive in there and keep telling him what's going on."

About 2 am, Rosie began to gag on her breathing tube. Henry was on mechanical breathing duty and ran over to shake Zora awake. She made her tired way to the kitchen and watched the cat for a while.

"She's made it," Zora finally stated.

She deflated the retention ring and quickly removed the breathing tube. Rosie retched once and began to breathe normally. Zora turned off the IV drip and pulled out the catheter in Rosie's vein.

"She'll be OK now," she whispered to Henry.

Henry was in no mood to whisper. "Yeee Hah!" he shouted. "YEEEEEEE-hah! Rosie's made it! We saved her!"

He hooted and danced around, waking everyone in the house except Bronwyn. They slowly roused themselves and gathered around the cat.

Rosie had rolled herself up into a normal resting posture and was looking around. Henry enthusiastically offered Marie's pink champagne to any takers and there was indeed a moment of general celebration. Everyone hoped that Rosie's recovery was a bellwether for Jeremy's recovery, too. Soon the party drifted back into an anxious slumber.

Morning arrived quickly, heralded by a 6 am call from Marie to say that Jeremy was in intensive care. He was in a life-threatening condition, but he was stable.

The party broke up then. Everyone had a day's work ahead of them. Rick and Zora showered and had breakfast at Marie's, and Zora took off on her rounds directly from there.

Rick and Bronwyn took Rosie back to the farm, saw that she was able to drink water from the bowl and nibble at her food, and that Engelbert ignored her as usual, then took off for Yarmouth to share the vigil there with Marie. Zora had an appointment down Meteghan way that afternoon and she planned to meet up with them about 5 pm.

What with Bronwyn's good breakfast, a travel banana and an overlap with nap time, Rick had a peaceful drive to Yarmouth.

The intensive care unit was brightly lit and bustling. Jeremy was in a screened-off cubicle. Possibly because Marie was sitting beside him, on first view Jeremy reminded Rick of a car in a repair shop receiving gas in its tank, air in its tires, a charge to its battery, an oil change and a computer analysis of its inner workings, all at the same time.

Marie looked up and whispered, "He may look dead, but he isn't."

She showed Rick the life monitors, with their little digital messages and lights and pulses and tracings. The monitors proclaimed very long slow heart beats with big intervals in between, but heart beats, nonetheless. They showed blood pressure almost too low for life, but not quite. They showed barely enough oxygen in the blood to keep the body from shutting down, but just enough. Jeremy's hand was still warm.

Marie said, "Jerry's heartbeats became totally erratic at about 2 am. The monitor lights flashed and alarms rang. The staff really seem to know what to do about hearts, though. They got him through the crisis and out the other side."

She shook her head. "They seem to think Jerry is improving, but I can't really see it."

Rick handed Bronwyn to Marie and took her place in the chair beside Jeremy. "Good morning, Jerry," he said. "I know this is a pretty scary time for you, but you are doing great; all your lights are on and we'll be driving home together before long. Rosie was knocked out just like you, but she is all better now. We took her to the farm to stay until you get home."

Nothing on the life monitors changed, but Rick hadn't expected a response. "Bronnie is here, too, Jerry. She was happy to see you when we came in. I'm going to sit her on the bed beside you for a few minutes."

Rick had no understanding whatsoever of the bond that had developed between Bronwyn and Jeremy almost from the day she was born, but he could see they both felt it, almost like magic.

There was just enough space between Jeremy's right arm and his body for Bronwyn to fit in. Rick lay her in this space. She settled in calmly for a while, then began fiddling with Jeremy's gown, hand and fingers, with a few coos and giggles and a cough and sneeze or two so that Jeremy would have had to be aware of her if any of his senses were working.

Rick bounced her lightly on Jeremy's stomach and chest, then decided Jeremy probably had had enough baby contact for the time being. Bronwyn needed food and a change, so he gave the chair back to Marie and went off with the baby gear to find a quiet lounge.

Marie had not slept in about 30 hours and was struggling to keep alert. As she sat in the chair fighting sleep, a man walked briskly into the cubicle and stopped at the foot of Jeremy's bed. "Hi Marie, I got a call from Monica this morning and she told me Jeremy and you were here. Sounds like a very upsetting turn of events. I was in Yarmouth overnight and when I heard I came right over to see how things are."

He looked a bit familiar, Marie thought. Her memory was not so sharp just then. "I'm sorry, I've forgotten your name."

"Billy, Billy Cleveland, from Annapolis. I'm going out with Monica."

As Billy was talking, the audio pulse from the heart monitor changed, increasing notably in frequency, and Jeremy's blood pressure moved up slightly.

"Thank you for coming, Billy," Marie said. "Jeremy is in a critical state right now, but he is receiving very good care here. Please let Monica know. He can't have visitors now, but perhaps in a few days."

Billy took the cue, looked Jeremy over briefly, wished them well, and departed.

Jeremy's heart rate and blood pressure really had gone up a notch. They stayed that way for five minutes or so and then slowly dropped back to their previous levels. "I think that man scared you Jerry," Marie said. "When you're all better again, maybe you can tell me why. Right now, don't worry about anything. You are safe here and we won't ever leave you alone."

Rick came back with Bronwyn fed and with some sandwiches for himself and for Marie. As they ate, Rick told Marie how things had gone since she and

Jeremy had left in the ambulance, how Rosie had re-covered and how Henry had re-ignited the party for a few minutes to celebrate.

When lunch was over, Rick said, "You really need to get some sleep now. Tonight will be another long vigil for you."

Marie nodded. "You're right. I'll find a hotel room and sleep as long as I can."

"Zora will show up late this afternoon," Rick said. "We can stay with Jeremy until 9 or 10 tonight."

As she prepared to leave, Marie asked, "Who is this Billy Cleveland guy, Monica's new beau? He stopped by to visit Jerry just after you went to change Bronwyn."

Rick told her what little he knew about Billy.

"When he began speaking, Jerry's heart rate and blood pressure jumped way up," Marie said. "I think Jerry knew his voice or maybe could see him and was frightened by him."

Marie departed, Bronwyn fell asleep, and Rick was left to his own thoughts. *Good question: who is this Billy Cleveland guy?*

Marie came back to the hospital at 9 pm. Nothing about Jeremy had changed.

After some discussion, it was decided that Rick, Zora and Bronwyn would go back home.

"I'll call around 8 tomorrow morning to update you," Marie said. "Then we can decide what more to do."

In Jeremy's cubicle, Marie had little to do in between the visits by various medical teams every twenty minutes or so. She held Jeremy's hand, squeezing it from time to time and saying something to him so he would know she was there.

As the unit became quiet in the early morning, Marie's thoughts drifted around to her old friend Rose, Jeremy's stepmother and guardian angel. Rose had done so much to rescue Jeremy from whatever it was that had befallen him at age 15, to find him a safe place to live, with Marie herself to keep an eye on him. Rose had feared for Jeremy's safety, feared his older brother might try to do him harm, and she had gone to such extremes to protect him. Now maybe it all had been undone by some bad food at a birthday party.

Marie could not help feeling at fault, somehow responsible for the chain of events that had led to this.

As she grieved to herself, Marie did not at first notice the new sensation in her hand, but then suddenly she did. Jeremy's hand was squeezing hers. It was slow and weak, but also too strong to be imagined. It came again, a slow, tighter squeeze.

"Jerry!" Marie exclaimed. "Jerry, squeeze my hand again, as hard as you can."

Jeremy's grip tightened once more around the back of her hand, and then relaxed.

She looked at the monitors. His heart rate was higher than before and so was his blood pressure. She leaned across him and looked into his face. Very slowly, his eyelids partially lowered and then rose again.

Marie burst into tears. He was back from the dead.

She grasped his shoulders and hugged him as closely as she dared with all his tubes and attachments, then pushed the call button.

Zora was about to disappear into her clinic at the back of the house to prepare for her first morning appointment when Marie's call came. She put her phone on speaker so Rick could hear too.

Jeremy had recovered in the night! An hour after he had first squeezed Marie's hand, the resident had taken out his breathing tube. Two hours more and he could stand and walk. The hospital wanted him to stay, to eat a meal, and to get a thorough medical checkup before departing. Marie expected they would be home by mid-afternoon.

The unit staff had thrown away the breathing tube because it was not the correct standard size. They were sending Lisa a new one.

17: Easy-peasy

Nobody died. A guy and his cat got sick and lived. The restaurant got a clean bill of health: no bad food anywhere. It was open for business again. The hospital staff thought Jeremy indeed had suffered shellfish poisoning, but there was no test to prove it for sure and, after he recovered, they had more urgent concerns. The few party-goers who had seen the paella pan on Jeremy's counter had a hard time avoiding the conclusion that something in that dish had nearly killed him, but there was no evidence to support their suspicion.

Rick Robichaud was losing sleep over that paella. If he had found Jeremy in his living room enjoying a bowl of that fabulous paella, Rick might well have joined him and had some, too. He might have tried a few of those little fish bits on Bronwyn. That paella could have killed everyone at the birthday party.

During one sleepless night, when Rick was again overwhelmed with anguish about Jeremy and the party and the paella, an image of Wade, his old university officemate, emerged out of the chaos of his thoughts. 'Green-goo Wade', they had called him. His passion was understanding sudden blooms of algae in the sea and all the animals they killed and didn't kill—fish yes, clams no, birds yes, starfish no...

For three years, Rick and Wade had shared a tiny graduate-student office in the depths of the Redpath Museum in Montreal. Wade had spent his summers trailing fine-meshed nets through the waters of the St Lawrence estuary, collecting jars and jars of greenish slime which he toiled each winter to identify and analyze. While Rick had abandoned his PhD program, Wade had gone all the way and finished his degree, and now he was somewhere in the national public health agency, in the lab that kept the country safe from all kinds of usual food poisons.

Rick had lost track of Wade, but the government on-line personnel directory had not. Next day, during his morning nap break from Bronwyn, Rick found Wade's number and called.

"Ricky-Ticky," Wade said excitedly. "How ya doin'? Still with Zori and the cheese farm?"

Rick said he was, and they brought each other up to speed on their lives in two sentences each.

"Wow! Papa Rick!" Wade said. "I bet you're a natural. She's a lucky little girl. You got two lucky girls!"

"Wade," Rick said, "I need your help. I've got a story to tell you."

He recounted the whole paella drama. "So, there it is. Case closed except we all could have died and one of us almost did."

"Two of you almost did, is what I heard," Wade said. "I know what you're thinking, and I know what you want, and I'll do it. What's your email? I'll send you the shipping instructions. Send the stuff to me personally and not just to the lab, okay? I'll have to put this one through the mill with some special excuses."

Rick had just enough time to pack the frozen samples of paella and get them off that morning with the courier who picked up the small cheese shipments. The guaranteed overnight delivery service got the package to Ottawa in just three days, almost a speed record for a package starting out from Lansdowne.

A close bond had developed among the coffee club members following Jeremy's birthday party. They had supported each other through that difficult event and had gained a new solidarity, like an army platoon that had survived a gruesome campaign. It had made their weekly gatherings even more important to them.

Today, the group was telling Monica once again that she and Billy had done nothing wrong, that whatever had happened was not their fault. Billy had not come today, and Monica was still very emotional and hard to convince. Bronwyn was being passed around among the baby-holders in the group and Rick was chatting with Rory at the counter when Rick's phone rang.

"Hey Ricky-Ticky, I've got some news for you."

Rick excused himself from Rory and went outside to take the call. "Hi, Wade. Thanks for calling. What's the news?"

"The news is that you've got a very smart wife, but

maybe that's not news to you. That rice sample had enough toxin in it to kill a small village, but that's not the best part."

Rick was stunned. "That's pretty big news, Wade. What's the best part?"

"I ran that stuff through for everything: shellfish toxins, paralytic, diarrheic, domoic, blue-greens, botulism A to F, the works. That rice had none of them, but it was chock full of tetrodotoxin."

"Tetrodotoxin? Like Tetraodon? Like pufferfish?"

"You're still the good fish man, Ricky. Yeah, pufferfish. Like that fugu fish people from some cultures eat for the buzz—just a little bit to get the tingle; a little more and you're dead. That's why we have a good test for it in this lab. It's the voodoo zombie poison, too. Ever read *The Serpent and the Rainbow*? You just need a smidge of tetrodotoxin, so your victim seems to die. You bury them alive and dig them up again that night, traumatized and stressed out like you wouldn't believe. Then you wreck their brains with some hardcore poisons and sell them off as zombie slaves. The critics say the book got the anthropology all wrong, but it sure got the tetrodotoxin right. It's the same effect as shellfish toxin, really, the way it works."

"How the hell does pufferfish get into a paella in a restaurant in Annapolis Royal?"

"I'm not the one who told you, but it didn't. We tested all the stuff sent in from that restaurant, stat-urgent, up half the night. Clean as a whistle, and there were no little flecks of fish in their paella, either."

"What the fuck?"

"Got to find that pufferfish, Ricky. I can't help you there. You're the fish man."

"Wade, you're a prince. What's your home address? I'm going to send you some terrific cheese."

"I'll have the wine ready and waiting, Ricky."

This is crazy. Rick knew something about pufferfish. They were among the tropical reef fish he was studying before he quit research. They're not very big when they're not all puffed up, and you won't find them in Nova Scotia either. It would have taken a pound or two to make all those little fish bits in the birthday paella. Too crazy.

But the whole business was crazy, "enough toxin to kill a small village" crazy. If those little fish bits weren't cooked all the way through, there might still be some good DNA inside, easy-peasy for the barcoders to figure out what they came from, if so.

What to do? Rick wondered. He went back to the group, snatched up Bronwyn and said their goodbyes. It was nap time for Bronnie and thinking time for Rick.

18: Rolling pictures

'Billy Cleveland' was tired of wondering how to get his brother to die. His plan had been perfect. The Korean drug dealer had got him the fish, and he'd gotten it all the way into Julian's fucking mouth, and then the goddamn cat and the goddamn vet and the goddamn nurse and now goddamn blubbering Monica. His phony persona was getting hard to keep in place.

It was time to get it done some other way; no more clever, fancy plots.

William Ferrante knew a few things about killing in untraceable ways. He'd been a pussy not to just do it right the first time, fifteen years ago. He needed to do it soon and then disappear again. He didn't want Wiss Artinian to track him down before he could make his own plans for Wiss.

He could take care of Julian; he just needed to decide on the time and place. He still had enough of that fish. He also had some pepper spray and neck-size plastic tighteners. What he didn't want was an audience.

Wiss Artinian was tired of wondering, too, tired of wondering where the fuck that cocksucker Ferrante was hiding. He knew he was close to him, though. Randall the forger had been very helpful, especially after they had given him some free dental work.

He was on the trail of 'Billy Cleveland' now. Hundred-dollar bills and a biker's way of asking generally got good information out of hotel clerks and car salesmen. Wiss could almost smell Ferrante now.

Rick could smell the sausages on his stove; they smelled spectacularly good. It was Lansdowne Highland's special fall bratwurst, fresh out of the sausage machine: no chemicals, no fake flavours, no binders; just plain sausages, short and thick.

His were going to join some new cabbage, leeks and potatoes in a late supper; Zora always got home late on Thursdays. The package in the fridge was to split between Marie and Jeremy, and when Bronwyn woke up, she and Rick made a quick delivery. Jeremy had been staying with Marie ever since he came back from the Yarmouth hospital, so they stopped there first.

Marie was still in her shop, working on her newest project, an electric car for herself. "Mechanics have to keep up with the times," she said. "The trouble with these electric cars is that nothing goes wrong with them and so there's nothing much to fix."

She said Jeremy had mostly stopped acting afraid of everything now and had moved back to his own place two days ago. "Put my sausages in the freezer compartment, if you don't mind, Ricky. I won't get to them for a few days. Tell Jerry to eat his right now or to freeze them, cooked or raw. We don't want any more food poisoning around here."

Jeremy was playing with Rosie, using an old sock tied to a string, when Rick and Bronwyn arrived. He looked stiff and awkward to Rick in this playmate role, but Rosie was totally into it. The more erratic the sock's movements the better.

Bronwyn reached for Jeremy, and Rick unpacked the sausages and laid them out on a plate, six fat glistening brats. He dug a food container out of a drawer and put it on the counter beside the sausages.

"You should cook these up right now and eat them, Jerry," he said. "Any you don't want to eat right now you can put in this container and freeze. Don't leave them on the counter, raw or cooked, for more than half an hour. They could become really poisonous if they sit out for a few hours in this warm house."

Jeremy came over to look at the sausages. He got out a frying pan, put it on his woodstove, and slid in all six of the brats.

"We're off, Jerry," Rick said. "Going home to eat the same thing. There are plenty more where these came from, so eat all you want."

Zora spent that evening making cookies and trying to keep up with her veterinary journals while she rocked Bronwyn to sleep. She got her into her crib finally and hauled Rick off to bed.

William Ferrante spent the evening packing up to move out of his apartment the next day and stay with Monica for what she didn't know would be his last night with her.

Wiss Artinian cruised the residential streets of Annapolis Royal in a cube van, looking for a Jeep with a certain license plate number, a little magnetic GPS tracker in his pocket, stopping now and then for a beer.

Zora's attention had gifted Rick a full night of peaceful sleep, but when the next night arrived, despite pizza and a movie and some very good Scotch from mama Lilian, his anxious obsessions returned in full force. In his tangled mind, images rolled into view like the lines of pictures on a slot machine, never aligning in any way that made sense or winning a prize. The lever came down again and again and again, and images just swirled by at random.

Zombies rolled past paella pans, pufferfish were swallowed by whales that leapt out of the water and fell back dead, ambulances ran over stumbling cats. The lever came down again, and there was Jeremy, then Green-goo Wade with his book of zombies, then legless Jérôme, all lined up together and pointing at each other.

This last line of images would not go away; it stuck in Rick's mind like the image on a frozen computer screen. It very slowly faded away without ever changing as Rick finally lapsed into an exhausted sleep.

Zora let Rick sleep in on Saturday morning. It was her day to be a full-time mom. When he finally got up, they all went to the café for coffee and pastries and to catch up on village news. She then dropped him back at the farm and headed off with Bronwyn to spend the afternoon with her mother.

Rick wanted to do some good, hard, physical work, so he decided to put the vegetable garden to bed for the winter. He mulched the garlic rows and strawberry patch and started hauling in and spreading manure by the wheelbarrow load.

He had worked up a really good sweat when suddenly the slot-machine image from his nightmare flashed into his mind and stopped him in his tracks. In two clear-eyed seconds, he saw it all.

- Jeremy is a voodoo zombie, like in Wade's book. He died at age 15 for no reason while in his elder brother's care. He was about to be cremated, aware and alive, but then was stolen away at the last minute, and he turned up 10 years later in Winnipeg, as if returned from the dead, with his brain scrambled.

- Jeremy's brother is William Ferrante, the kid on the motorcycle who nearly died of shellfish poisoning himself in 1999. He knew what that poisoning was like; he knew what he was doing. He did it to his brother

- William had just poisoned Jeremy for a second time, like what the shrink said about Jérôme. Not once but twice, and in the same way, and maybe for the same reason.

- William Ferrante wants Jeremy dead. He must have gotten those fish bits into the paella. But only Billy Cleveland or Monica Jeffries could have put those fish bits into the paella. Jeremy is afraid of Billy Cleveland. Cleveland must be William Ferrante.

Shit! It was 3 pm. This Ferrante must be some kind of psychopath bent on killing Jerry. Jerry was alone at home, totally vulnerable. Ferrante was sure to try again, and what about Monica?

19: You'll hear the first click

William Ferrante had decided that Saturday would be the best day. The ATVs would be out in force, making plenty of noise in the back country, so people in Morganville would ignore what was happening in the road. All his stuff was in the Jeep. In the end, he'd thrown the fish in the garbage; he would use a faster and more certain means to put Julian away.

He had no further use for Monica; he'd be far away before he would look for a bed tonight. Monica was in the shower but came out just as Billy finished his coffee. It was time to make sure she knew it was over.

He stood up and punched her in the face. Monica collapsed to the floor with an astonished scream. He reached down and punched the other side of her face as best he could. Lots of blood from her nose this time.

He straightened up. "I'm out of here," he said. "Don't try to find me or help anyone else try, or you'll wish you hadn't." It was best to be clear about such matters. It was good to feel like himself again.

He walked out the door and drove off to Morganville.

As he had predicted, there was plenty of ATV and other traffic on the Morganville Road. He slipped into Jeremy's hidden driveway, grabbed his papers and walked quickly to the kitchen door.

Jeremy was standing in the kitchen. He looked up when William strode in, and froze in place.

William was in no mood for pretensions of gentleness. "Sit down in that chair, Julian," he bellowed. "Now!"

He bristled with genuine menace, and Jeremy sat down submissively, looking away, cowed by the old sibling dominance.

"You're not getting away this time," William continued loudly. "You stole my money and you're giving it back. You sign this right now or you won't sign anything ever again. You sign it, then maybe we can talk for a while, maybe take a little walk in your woods."

He pulled a thick document out of a folder and threw it and a pen down in front of Jeremy. "You sign that 'Julian Ferrante,' not fucking 'Jeremy Franklin.'"

Jeremy sat staring at the paper and pen while his brother looked around the kitchen as if inspecting a newly conquered kingdom. "Get me something to eat," he barked. "I missed breakfast."

Jeremy sat up straighter in his chair and looked at William for a long moment. Then he rose slowly and took down a frying pan from the top of the warming oven of the wood stove. The pan contained two cooked sausages, nicely warmed by the rising heat from the stove as they had been since they were cooked almost two days before. He looked at the sausages in the pan for another long moment, then at his brother again, and finally set the frying pan down in front of him.

"Fork," William snapped. "And I want more than this."

Jeremy dutifully found a fork and got out some bread and peanut butter. William pushed the peanut butter aside.

"I don't eat this shit," he said. He had already eaten one sausage and he wrapped the second in a slice of bread and devoured it, too. "Sign that fucking paper."

He picked up a long metal poker that was lying beside the stove and banged it on the table in front of Jeremy, by way of emphasis. Jeremy sat expressionless, staring at the paper.

A car pulled into Jeremy's driveway and manoeuvred around Billy's Jeep into the back yard. Lisa Willson hopped out with her medical bag and hurried to the kitchen door.

"Good morning, Jerry," she said cheerfully. "Whose car is that?"

She took off her coat in the entry way and came into the kitchen, seeing Ferrante for the first time. "Oh, it's yours, Billy. I didn't recognize it. I'm actually driving Jerry's car now, until Marie gets our replacement put together. She says it's almost ready."

Ferrante tried not to let his rage and displeasure at Lisa's arrival show through his thin veneer of civility.

"I'm sorry to interrupt your visit," Lisa said. "I'm here to give Jerry an examination as a follow-up to his food poisoning episode and I'm on a tight schedule. Its going to take us at least an hour. I'm sure Jerry won't mind if you stay until we're done, if you'd rather not leave and then come back later."

Ferrante thought for a moment. "I'll stay, he said. "I'll just take a nap on the living room couch."

He went into the living room and Lisa began a complete neurological examination, followed by a lot of yes/no questions that Jeremy answered very slowly. Ears, eyes, breathing, vision, hearing…

In the end, it took almost two hours to get through it all, but finally they were done.

"Jerry, you're as fit as a fiddle, 100%. Nothing left over from that bad meal. You tell Marie that I was here today and that I said you are 100% okay."

Lisa packed up her bag and headed for the entryway, but then remembered Billy Cleveland. She popped her head into the living room. "We're all done, Billy," she said. "Thanks for being so patient."

Ferrante seemed to open his eyes with difficulty. His face looked odd, slack-skinned around the eyes and upper cheeks, which was all she could see above his beard.

"You're looking tired, Billy. Better use the weekend to catch up on rest."

She gave Jeremy's shoulder a goodbye squeeze, grabbed her coat and was gone.

Ferrante struggled to his feet and tried to resume

his alpha male posture, but he couldn't quite manage it. He figured he must have gotten into a deep sleep, and he tried to shake it off. He shuffled into the kitchen.

"Sit in that goddamn chair and sign that fucking paper," he commanded.

He sat down himself to wait out Julian's turtle-slow ways and gazed absently out the window toward the driveway and the road beyond. A white cube van almost came to a stop in the road at the end of the driveway, but then continued eastward.

"Make me some coffee," he demanded with effort.

Jeremy rose slowly and put a kettle on the stove. He went to a cupboard and came to the table with a cup and a spoon and the jar of instant coffee Mel kept there to drink when he visited.

"I guess that'll have to do," Ferrante grumbled. "Hurry the fuck up."

But the fire was low, and the kettle required a good ten minutes to start making the noises that suggested its intent to boil. Finally steam began to emerge from it and Jeremy poured boiling water into the cup.

Ferrante didn't open the coffee jar and stir in a spoonful. Instead, he fell off his chair and lay sprawled on the floor, his eyelids half closed, his lips loose, his mouth askew. He tried once to rise but couldn't.

Jeremy sat in his chair, watching his brother on the floor. William seemed unable to move or speak.

After ten minutes or so, Jeremy gathered up the

paper and pen from the table and put them into the firebox of the stove. They burned vigorously for a minute or two.

There was a sudden roar and throb of powerful, unmuffled engines. Two massive, chopper-style motorcycles, one with a passenger, rolled in and parked behind William's car. All three men wore leather and had beards, boots and tattoos.

The solo rider ran directly to Jeremy's front door, and through its small window Jeremy glimpsed the face of Wiss Artinian grimacing at the door handle. Jeremy was 100 yards into the forest and still running fast before Wiss succeeded in kicking in the door.

Wiss and his buddies strode into the house and found Ferrante on the kitchen floor, gasping for breath at long intervals. Wiss kicked him in the ribs. "I came here to kill you, Ferrante, you motherfucker. Don't you die before I get the chance. What's happened to you? Did you have a coronary when you saw I'd caught you? You threaten Wiss Artinian, bad things happen."

He kicked him twice more. "I hope you can hear me, fuckhead. Whatever's happened to you here, you don't have to worry about dying from it. I'll take care of that for you right now. Let's go."

Wiss grabbed William by one ankle and a gang member took him by the other. They dragged him out the front door and down the steps and threw him into his Jeep. They found his keys and roared away east on the Morganville Road, two choppers and a Jeep, to the roadside clearing two miles down the road where they had left their van.

Wiss could hardly contain his disappointment that Ferrante was already practically dead. During their search for him, Wiss had thought of several creative ways to make his death slow and painful.

They hauled him out of the Jeep and watched him for signs of life. It seemed he was no longer breathing.

Wiss straddled him, a pistol in his hand. "Okay, Ferrante," he said. "This will be our last conversation. I hope you can still hear me. I'm going to put a bullet through each of your eyeballs, my little signature, you know, just so the folks who count will understand that you never mess with Wiss Artinian. You'll hear the first click; that's me cocking the gun. You might not hear the second click even though it'll be a lot louder."

Wiss leaned over and shot Billy in the left eye, then repositioned himself and shot him in the right.

They had parked in a clearing just off the road that must once have been the yard of a house. There was an old well with a rotten cover and a long drop down to the water. They threw William into it headfirst.

They got some Jerry cans of gasoline out of the van, doused the Jeep abundantly inside, and threw in a match. They watched the fire with satisfaction, then loaded their choppers into the van and drove away, first to the Halifax airport to drop off Wiss and his lieutenant, and then to start the long, solo drive back to Winnipeg for Henry, the gang rookie.

~

Rick was in a panic. He raced for his truck, calling Roger Laliberty as he did so. "Roger, I'm going to Jeremy Franklin's place because I am sure someone will try to kill him today, maybe already has. Can you meet me there? I'll explain later."

"I'm on my way," Roger said. Rick already was speeding down Clark Road and arrived at Jeremy's ahead of Roger.

What to do? Go in and get killed, too? I guess so.

He walked cautiously to the kitchen door, knocked loudly and stepped quickly aside, like in the movies. No response. He opened the door and called, "Jerry?" Nothing.

Rick took a deep breath and walked in. The wood-stove fire was burning, and the place was nice and warm. In the living room, he discovered that the front door had been forced open. Otherwise, there was no evidence of violence, but Jeremy was not at home.

Roger arrived and Rick went out to his patrol car.

"Anything wrong here, Rick?"

"Somebody has forced open the front door and Jeremy isn't home. Nothing else unusual that I can see."

"I got another call on the way over here, a car on fire on this road just past the communications tower. I'll come back as soon as I can, or send someone. Can you stay here until then?"

Rick nodded and Roger left in a spray of gravel.

He waited in the kitchen. Before long, a fire truck wailed its way east along the road.

Rick looked around the house. He wondered who had wanted a cup of instant coffee in Jeremy's kitchen, and why they had poured out the water but never made the coffee. He wondered why the steel poker was on the kitchen table.

As he sat pondering it all, there was a scrabbling sound in one of the banks of kitchen drawers and Rosie came crawling out from under it. Rick knew that this was her place to hide from visiting dogs; she could get into the next-to-bottom drawer from behind through a damaged panel. He wondered what she had been hiding from.

Rosie came out cautiously, rubbed herself against Rick's leg, sniffed around and inspected the kitchen and living room, and then went to her food bowl.

Rick's phone rang. It was Lisa Willson. "Ricky, where are you?"

"In Jerry's kitchen."

"I was just calling you to ask you to go there and see if Jerry is okay. It's so awful. Monica called me to come over; she sounded terrified and when I got there, I found her all beaten up. She didn't want to go to the clinic or to say who did it but finally she told me it was her boyfriend Billy. This morning, he told her he was leaving her, and he beat her up. But I was at Jerry's before she called me, and Billy was there when I arrived, and he was still there when I left two hours later. Is Jerry okay?"

Rick said, "Jerry isn't here now, so I really don't know how he is. The RCMP are coming soon. I'm staying here until they arrive."

They rang off, Lisa more worried now than when she had called.

Roger came back after about forty minutes. "That car has burned completely. It could be a Jeep, but I can't be sure. We'll be able to read the serial number once the frame cools down. Also, there's something deep down a well near the burned car. With my flashlight, it looks like the bottom of a pair of boots."

Rick took a deep breath. "Roger, I didn't tell you this, but you are going to find out that there is a dead man down that well. It could be Jerry, but Jerry never wears boots. I'm pretty sure you'll find that it's William or Billy Cleveland and that the burnt car is his car. You'll find out later that his real name is William Ferrante. You'll find out that he was out to kill Jeremy for some reason and that he put the poison in that birthday party paella that nearly did kill him. You'll find out that the poison he put in the paella was the flesh of a kind of pufferfish that is full of stuff called tetrodotoxin and that he put in enough to kill everyone at the party. If the Mounties search his apartment in Annapolis right away, they might even find some of that fish, in the fridge or the freezer, or in the garbage, probably only a few ounces, raw white fish meat."

Roger was having trouble taking in all this inform-ation. "Can you verify any of this?"

"You're going to verify it all yourself soon. But there's more. You are going to find out that this Ferrante was into crime in various ways, and maybe that's why he's down that well. Jeremy could never have gotten him there. You're going to learn that Ferrante was dating Monica Jeffries and that he beat her up this morning. Lisa Willson will tell you that she found Ferrante with Jeremy here in this house today at noon and that he was still here when she left at about 2 pm. In the end, you're going to want to charge Ferrante with assault and with attempted murder. But he's already dead."

20: Must be slipping

Only the dead slept well that Saturday night. Marie, Mel, Zora and Rick were desperate to know where Jeremy might be. He had not come home, and he had not come to Marie's house or the farm.

They had gathered at his house, to wait and to hope. Bronwyn fussed and cried and would not be comforted, perhaps from all the tension in the air. Lisa and Rory had brought Monica back to their place, partly to help manage her injuries, since she would not go to the clinic, but mostly to support her through her personal trauma.

Lisa got a social services counsellor on the phone, and the two hours she talked with Monica seemed to bring Monica back from the brink.

Roger Laliberty slept poorly in his patrol car at the well, where he had to wait until noon on Sunday for a homicide team to arrive.

Rick, Zora and Bronwyn were off to a wedding on Sunday, way down on Brier Island. Mel decided to move into Jeremy's house for a few days, so someone would always be there in case Jeremy returned. He began his vigil on Sunday morning.

The homicide team made a sweep of Jeremy's

house that afternoon, paying particular attention to the bashed-in front door. The lead investigator had interviewed Lisa and Monica, and he insisted that he must also speak with Jeremy. He found it suspicious that no one knew where Jeremy was.

Mel tried to explain Jeremy to the investigator, his unusual nature, but he could see his effort had no useful effect. Mel said he would try to find Jeremy and would call the RCMP if he was successful.

As dusk arrived in the late afternoon, Mel sat in Jeremy's kitchen, drinking his own instant coffee. Constable Roger Laliberty had stopped in, hoping to find Rick to confirm to him that the homicide team had just hauled the body of Billy Cleveland out of that well and sent it off for autopsy.

As Mel mused about things after Roger departed, it came into his mind that Jeremy might have gone to his camp on Crouse Lake, a place Jeremy knew and could get to himself and hide and feel safe, a place where no one else would likely ever go. Seven miles through the bush was nothing to Jeremy and he could have walked on a back road part of the way.

The more he thought about it, the more convinced Mel became that Jeremy was at his camp and that he should go there right away.

Mel phoned Marie. "I think Jerry is hiding out at my camp and I should go there right now. Can you take over my watch at his house and maybe bring me some food to take along? There's nothing to eat at the camp."

"Can you really get there by yourself in the dark

and the cold?"

"There's no ice yet. My canoe's on my truck ready to go. I can do it."

"I'll be over in 15 minutes."

Three hours later, as he lifted the canoe over the beaver dam up to lake-level, Mel could just make out a dim light coming from a window in his camp across the lake. He looked at his phone and saw it still had a weak signal, and quickly sent a text message to Marie: "He's here."

When the canoe grounded noisily on the small beach in front of the camp, Mel heard the back-door snap closed on its spring. He quickly called out, "It's me Jerry: Mel. No one else, just me. Come help me."

Footsteps approached from the forest edge and Jeremy was quickly beside him, pulling out the packs and lifting the canoe up clear of the water, carrying everything into the cabin in almost a frenzy of effort.

A fire was burning, and the camp was warm. Jeremy was standing in the middle of the room, dirty, dishevelled, looking exhausted and with terror in his eyes. He was shaking.

"It's all right Jerry," Mel said. "No one's going to hurt you here."

Jeremy slowly sat down on a chair at the table, still looking almost pleadingly at Mel, still shaking.

Mel fished around in the back of a low cupboard and came out with a plastic bottle of black rum. He put two water glasses on the table and filled each halfway. "Drink some of this," he said as he sat down across from Jeremy and sipped from his own glass.

Jeremy sipped also, then quickly drank most of his double shot.

Mel tapped Jeremy's glass with his own and said, "That's good. Finish it."

He picked one of Marie's food parcels off the floor and unpacked two big, thick sandwiches. He took a half sandwich off the top for himself and pushed the rest over to Jeremy. "You got almost two days' worth of eating to catch up on: better get going."

Jeremy needed no urging; he inhaled the sandwiches.

Mel fished around in the food package again and came up with half a pie. He added a fork and pushed it over to him.

Jeremy had stopped shaking but still looked like a scared rabbit. Mel added some more rum to their glasses.

"That Billy guy is dead, Jerry, he got killed yesterday. Were you afraid of him?"

Jeremy looked down at his rum, took a small sip, then raised his eyes to meet Mel's. He made one long affirmative nod.

"Well, that's over now," Mel said.

Jeremy looked at Mel again and slowly shook his head "No."

"What do you mean? Is there someone else you're afraid of?"

Jeremy made a slow nod yes again, then looked away from Mel and took another drink of his rum. Very slowly, he said the word, "Artinian." Then he whipped his eyes back to Mel's, stood up and nearly screamed, "Wiss," with an urgent tone of panic in his voice. He threw himself face down on his bunk and didn't move again until morning.

Mel sat at the table, sipping down first his own rum and then what was left of Jeremy's. "Artinian" and "Wiss": what did those words mean? Whatever it was, he had never seen Jeremy so terrified. He figured he and Jeremy should stay another day at camp, to let Jeremy and everything else settle down.

There was a big pile of firewood rounds that needed to be split and stacked, and between that work and Marie's gourmet meals and naps, soon it already was the next day and time to leave.

While Jeremy carried things down to the canoe, Mel made his usual rounds of the cabin, putting things away, mouse-proofing food and setting his mouse trapline, checking critical supplies like lamp oil, matches and toilet paper, and checking that his guns and ammunition were well hidden. He looked down their barrels to make sure they were sparking clean.

To his dismay, the .30-30 was filthy. Did he really forget to clean it after he and Jeremy had shot at that old snag in the spring? He must be slipping. Mel got out his cleaning rods and brushed and oiled and wiped out the fine old barrel.

The box of shells had been left beside the rifle. "Not supposed to do that either," he chided himself.

He concealed the now-clean rifle and carried the shells to a different hiding place in a cupboard. As he did so, he noticed that three of the 10 shells in the box were missing—another puzzle; he and Jeremy had only shot off two, hadn't they?

For a moment he entertained the idea that someone had come to his camp, found his hidden gun and shells and fired off one round, leaving the gun dirty and a third shell missing. He dismissed the idea just as quickly. It was far more likely that he and Jeremy had fired the gun three times and that he just had forgotten.

They were off and, with a tail wind on the lake, they were back at Jeremy's house in Morganville in a record hour and a half. The next day the lakes froze, ending the canoe season until the spring.

21: *Lagocephalus lunaris*

The homicide investigators discovered a complicated case at the bottom of that well. The medical examiner reported that the victim had been shot twice
through the brain, once through each eye, but that he
had been dead before the shots were fired: there
was no bleeding along the bullet tracks. She found
lethal amounts of botulism toxin in the recently-
eaten sausage in his stomach, and in his blood.

The investigators found that Billy Cleveland had
carried forged papers and an identity stolen from a
deceased homeless man in Vancouver. They found
that he had opened a bank account in Windsor, Nova
Scotia with a big cheque from the account belonging,
through a labyrinth of numbered accounts, to a person named William Ferrante, whom they were, as
yet, unable to locate.

This William Ferrante had a police record of ar-
rest and release without charge as part of a motorcycle gang in Winnipeg in 2001. They found that the
Ontario Provincial Police had some hair from a hair-
brush found in a garbage can outside a rental home
in the Town of Fergus that had been blown up with
gelignite some weeks ago, two days after a William

Ferrante had moved out. Some of that hair was on its way to the RCMP crime lab, to see if its DNA matched that of the man down the well. They were still working on fingerprints.

An elderly gentleman who lived in the last house at the east end of Morganville, and who had driven down to see the burned-out car after the firefighters had left, told Roger that he'd seen two big motorcycles carrying three 'Hells Angels' drive past his place, heading west, mid-afternoon on Saturday and then back again later, with a jeep in between them. They'd never driven past again, and he didn't know where they could have gone. The Morganville Road was a dead end.

Mel called the RCMP when he returned to Morganville with Jeremy, as he had promised to do. The lead investigator asked the local detachment to interview him and, as usual, Roger Laliberty was sent to do it.

Roger knew a little of Jeremy's odd ways and, with Mel's help, he got from him that Billy Cleveland had come to his house on Saturday morning, and had stayed while Lisa Willson was with him for about two hours, that some bikers had come to his house not long after Lisa had left, and that Jeremy had run away to Mel's camp as soon as he saw the bikers.

The homicide team was not interested in the food poisoning from which Jeremy had recovered, but Roger was. When the forensic squad searched Billy Cleveland's apartment in Annapolis Royal, Roger asked them to look hard for any kind of fish, raw or cooked. They found a few ounces of stale raw fish in the garbage container under the kitchen sink.

Because Roger had been such a good sport on his overnight vigils at crime scenes lately, and because he seemed to want it so much, the team sent the fish off to the crime lab to determine what species of fish it was, and to send some on to the public health agency to check for food-borne toxins.

By the end of the week, life was settling down again. Jeremy was not yet comfortable in his own house, but he seemed relaxed and his normal self again living on the Robichaud-Cromwell farm.

Bronwyn got her first teeth, which made both her and Zora cross. Marie finished rebuilding the replacement car she had engineered for Lisa and Rory, and Rory got two more rejection notices from literary magazines. Monica's employers gave her two weeks' paid leave to help her pull her life back together.

Rick was making good use of Jeremy as a house guest. When they found the time, they ran year-end apples through an old cider press he had bought at an auction and restored to function. In the evenings, Bronwyn was so content to be with Jeremy that Rick occasionally had a little free time on his hands. He used it to obsess and worry over the events still spinning around Jeremy.

What brought motorcycle gangsters to Jeremy's door? Ferrante was on a motorcycle tour of Nova Scotia when he got shellfish poisoning way back when, touring with another guy, the newspaper said.

Who was that other guy?

Rick felt challenged. Who *was* that guy? Maybe it was important. He knew he would never get the name of a patient treated twenty years ago just by asking medical records at the Queen Elizabeth II medical centre in Halifax. But maybe it had been an unusual case at the time; maybe they wrote it up in a medical journal, the way university docs often do.

He tried searching some science databases he still had access to, using search words like shellfish poisoning, PSP, Nova Scotia, 1999, Ferrante.

One article popped up, published in 1999 in a journal quaintly entitled *Morbidity and Mortality Weekly Report*. It was the same story as in the *Annapolis County Spectator* but with way more technical detail. At the very end, there were some acknowledgements, including, "to W. Artinian and W. Ferrante, for their cooperation."

Bingo! Rick was excited at his find. He quickly pulled up the article he had found before in the Winnipeg *Free Press* that listed Ferrante among a bunch of local motorcycle gang members. At the top of that alphabetical list was a "Wiss Artinian."

So? Or maybe just, so what? That was 19 years ago, and Ferrante seemed to have been in Ontario, not in Manitoba, for most of the intervening years.

Rick's phone beeped the arrival of a text message from an Ottawa number. The message was short: "Lagocephalus lunaris. loaded. same as paella. report tomorrow."

So, Wade had gotten Roger's fish sample. Rick recognized the fish by its Latin name; it was the "Lunartail Puffer", from southern Asia somewhere. He knew nothing else about it, but he quickly determined that the Internet knew a lot.

The species was famous for having lots of tetrodotoxin throughout its muscles while other puffer fish had it mostly in their guts and gonads. The lunartail was never to be eaten since no part of it was safe.

Well, one mark for Ferrante: he chose the right species of pufferfish to use to kill people.

This was interesting new detail, but it only confirmed what Rick already knew. Wiss Artinian was completely new to Rick, but likely the name meant nothing.

Jeremy was still rocking Bronwyn. Rick figured he had time for one more Internet query. He put "W. Artinian" into his search engine, pressed "go," and immediately got a flashing special breaking news story from the CBC.

The cement-bunker clubhouse of a gang called the C-Company Motorcycle Club in Winnipeg had just been blown off the face of the earth, sending debris raining down on parked cars and nearby buildings. Several people were known to have been inside at the time, including the gang leader, one Wiss Artinian.

Rick read the story again and tried to imagine where it could fit in the current murder drama. Hadn't Jeremy's stepmother Rose found Jeremy in Winnipeg after he was supposed to have been dead for ten years? And Jeremy had told Mel and Roger that he had run away from his house that Saturday when some motorcycles had arrived.

Rick knew that Jeremy could read perfectly well when he wanted to. "Jerry," he said, "what do you think of this?"

He showed him the news story, took Bronwyn and offered Jeremy his chair. Jeremy glanced through it quickly, but then stared at the screen with riveted attention. He seemed to be reading the story over and over.

Finally, he rose slowly from the chair with an undefinable expression on his face. He walked directly to his bedroom and slept without waking for 21 hours.

The C-Company rookie, Henry, heard the same breaking news story on the radio as he drove the cube van along the endless stretch of the Trans-Canada Highway from Thunder Bay west toward Kenora. That bomb probably was meant to kill him, too. Maybe Randall Pickford hadn't appreciated the free dentistry they'd given him. They should have done more than just pull out his teeth.

Henry turned off the highway onto a side road and found a place to park the van that was not too close to anything. He changed into his regular street clothes. Inside the van, he cut the gas lines of the two choppers and poured out all the gasoline remaining in the Jerry cans. He saved a little to half fill a pop bottle.

He put a rag in the bottle as a stopper, waited for it to wick up some gas, lit it with his lighter and threw the bottle into the open rear door of the van. There was a satisfying explosion and immediately a raging fire.

Henry walked back to the highway and began hitch-hiking east, away from Winnipeg.

22: A rumour going around

The ballistics team found 20-odd bits of lead in Rex Cheever's wall. Two of them had patterned scratches they possibly could match to the gun barrel through which the bullet had been fired. The bullet had been an old kind of 150-grain hollow-point .30-30, designed to expand on impact and make a large hole in its target. It had broken apart when it encountered Rex Cheever's neck bones and so had made an extra-large hole in the wall behind.

Based on trajectory estimates, the shot must have come into the room through the 6-inch-tall space of the open side window. The shooter must have been just outside the house and very close to the opening to make an accurate shot through that narrow space.

A group of six special investigation officers, armed with warrants, descended on the village one Monday morning, knocking on doors, asking to see all firearms, taking the few .30-30s in people's possession away for testing. They interviewed family, neighbours, community leaders and some residents at random about people whom Rex Cheever might have harmed, and they doubled down with questions on all such people thus identified. Community leaders told the officers that Rex had a reputation for violence against many people, but they could not come up with the names of individuals who had been harmed.

Zora and Rick were high on the officers' list because of Rex's attack on Rick and Bronwyn. Melvin Prime had a reputation for standing up to Rex from time to time, so he also got the third degree. Like Rick and Zora, the only gun in his home was a shotgun, unused for years.

They interviewed Jeremy, because he was a friend of Mel's and people had heard Rex insult him in public from time to time. Jeremy offered no insights and owned no guns at all.

Purley Jordan, Rex's nearest neighbour, told the officers that if he knew who the shooter was, he wouldn't tell them and that they should leave the village alone. For expressing this sentiment, Purley's house was given a particularly thorough search and he was told that he may have uttered a threat to obstruct justice. Purley said that if the police knew anything about justice, they would all just go home.

The few people who knew that Rex had assaulted Lisa Willson the same day he himself was shot felt it was not a story worth repeating. Lisa and Rory had been through enough.

The police wanted to know where each of their interviewees was the night Rex Cheever was shot. Mel had been down Digby Neck, visiting a nephew for the night. Rick and Zora were at home, a fact the small night shift in la fromagerie attested to. All the neighbours had been home with their families.

Only Jeremy was without some witness as to his whereabouts that night. When they asked where he had been, all he would say was, "Woods."

Rick was able to corroborate that, when Jeremy had arrived at the farm the next evening, he looked like he had indeed just spent a few days in the woods, but he could not say more than this.

The officers searched Jeremy's house thoroughly, but found nothing of interest.

Rex's house and land also came in for some renewed attention. The family had closed the side window, cleaned up the mess in the living room and shut the house down for the winter. Otherwise, it had been left alone.

The new police attention was on exactly where the shooter would have been when he or she fired the shot. To shoot through the narrow window opening, it seemed the shooter would have had to stand a couple of feet off the ground, on a chair or a step ladder or some other object placed only two or three feet from the house.

They searched the house and outbuildings for anything that might have served this purpose, found an old stool in a tool shed and took fingerprints.

They searched the ground in front of the window with sensitive metal detectors, hoping to find an ejected shell from the fatal shot. If they found the shell, they might be able to match scratches on its surface to the chamber of the rifle which had discharged it.

Constable Roger Laliberty was at the periphery of these investigations. The Digby detachment had designated him to be their official liaison with the investigative teams responding to the two recent murders in his village. His main job was to facilitate the teams' work and to stay out of their way. He seldom was asked for his opinions on anything and so he mostly kept them to himself.

Roger recognized a member of this new ballistic investigation team as one of the officers who had followed the tracker dogs on the day of Rex's murder. When the metal detectors found nothing in the vicinity of Rex's house, Roger suggested they sweep out further in the field and some distance along the general direction in which the dogs had initially followed a scent from the field edge. Two metal sweepers headed into the woods with the former dog handler as guide.

Roger stood at the edge of the field, watching them work their way to the southeast, then turned to look at Rex's house. With his binoculars, he could see straight through the lower edge of the side window to the big hole where the wall behind Rex's chair had been cut away. *Rex's neck would have been right along this same line of sight*, he thought.

Rick was panting his way up the steep hill of Lansdowne Road from Bear River, pushing Bronwyn in the runner's stroller back home after a mail run, when he heard a car approach from behind, slow down and draw even with him. It was Roger.

Rick stopped and Roger rolled down his window.

"If you get in any better shape, I may have to start giving you speeding tickets," he said.

They chatted about nothing for a few minutes, then Roger said, "There's a rumour going around that the Halifax Office is starting to think Jeremy Franklin might be the prime suspect in the Cheever case."

Rick looked worried. "Why is that?" he asked.

"For the wrong reason, probably. He can't account for where he was that night and they think his odd ways are just a cover."

Roger paused. "They don't seem to know that he can shoot an egg out of the air twenty times in a row."

He looked at Rick. "It would be hard on Jeremy if they were to find some real evidence to go on."

He paused. "Oops! Gotta go," he said." Staff meeting in 15 minutes."

He eased his patrol car ahead of Rick and Bronwyn and sped off toward Digby.

Late that evening, Melvin Prime called. "Is Jerry still staying with you folks?"

"He's over with Marie now," Rick said, "He's working himself back to feeling safe in his own home again."

"I need to talk with you without Jerry around," Mel said. "Can I drive up to the farm right now?"

Bronwyn was going to be up for at least another two hours and Zora already was asleep, so Rick told Mel to come right over.

When he arrived, Mel got right to the point. "Have

you heard what they're sayin' in town? They're sayin' that the cops are gonna come back and start searching all the camps around for guns and spent shells. Any .30-30s they find, they'll take and test."

Rick's and Mel's eyes locked for a moment. Rick said, ""Are you thinking what I'm thinking?"

"If you're thinking that Jerry shot Rex Cheever with my old .30-30, then I am."

They sat in silence again for a while. Bronwyn was starting to wriggle impatiently. "Do you know about Lisa?" Rick asked.

Mel nodded. "She told me herself one day when I mentioned that she seemed to be in a hell of a mess for just side-swiping a rock with her car. She said Jerry knew and so I maybe should know, too. She asked me to keep it quiet."

Bronwyn was done with sitting on Rick's lap. Rick lay down on the floor and started bouncing her up in the air off his stomach. She giggled and laughed.

Mel sighed, "Before we left camp last week, I checked my two guns out there. The .30-30 had been fired since I last cleaned it and a shell was missing that I never shot. Jeremy's about the only person besides me who even knows that gun exists."

Rick worked Bronwyn up and down in the air for another minute. "Shall we go tonight?"

"Yes sir," Mel replied.

They looked at the clock; it was just midnight.

"Better wait an hour or two," Mel said.

At two o'clock on Thursday morning, Rick woke Zora to tell her he had to be away for the rest of the night. If Bronwyn awoke, she would have to go to her.

"It's to help Jerry," he said. "I'll explain when I get back."

Zora woke up enough to look hard at Rick. "Are you going to do anything dangerous?"

"No, I'm not."

She pushed up for a kiss, moved the baby monitor to her side of the bed and settled back to sleep.

It was a half hour drive to the end of the Lake Joli Road. From there they kept going on a forestry track until they were as close to Mel's camp as they could get. With flashlights and GPS, they reached the cabin in another hour.

Mel retrieved his .30-30 and they retraced their path to the truck and back to the farm.

"What can a blacksmith make out of a rifle?" Rick asked as they drove along.

"I been thinking," Mel said. "I can cut it into pieces and hammer each piece flat, no barrel left to test that way. Later I can split the flats for horseshoe lengths or something. Do the same for the bolt and the chamber, and just burn up the stock."

When they arrived at the farm, Rick said he could hide the rifle where no one would look for it. "You'll need help at the forge when the time comes and we both need some sleep. When can we do it?"

"How about Friday morning, say 10 am when hardly anyone's around?"

It was agreed. Rick took the rifle and Mel drove off.

23: Do you ever give lessons?

It was 5:30 in the morning. Rick walked out to Ferdinand's corral.

Ferdinand was the biggest, scariest-looking Highland bull anyone had ever seen. Neither cop nor robber would ever enter his pen voluntarily.

Rick climbed over the fence, scratched Ferdinand's forehead and stashed the rifle deep under the hay in the bull's round-bale feeder. Fortunately, if he knew you, Ferdinand also was a sweetheart, most of the time.

That done, Rick hoped he might get in an hour of sleep before Bronwyn called.

It was Jérôme Weaver, not Bronwyn, who woke Rick later that morning. To give Rick a little more sleep, Zora had taken Bronwyn to the clinic for as long as she and her clientèle could put up with her.

Jérôme knocked loudly on the door at 8:30. "There's a pair of RCMP officers with a warrant to search the dairy and farm buildings. For weapons, they say."

"Okay, we'll cooperate with them in any way they wish," Rick said. "I'll be over right away."

As he was getting dressed, first Marie and then

Mel phoned to say that some Mounties had just turned up at their places to search their shops. It seemed like another police sweep was underway.

Steady, steady, Rick thought. No one had anything to hide, except him.

Before he went out, he retrieved Bronwyn from Zora. Bronnie in a backpack might soften whatever criminal image of him the policemen might have in their minds.

The Mounties were polite but formal and said they must look everywhere.

"I'll go with you, then," Rick said, "so you can get access to whatever you want to see."

They had a field day in the small barn that served as tool shed and shop. There were long, hard, linear objects in every corner and on every shelf. They scrutinized the cheese-making rooms, under the strict oversight and occasional reprimand of the cheese makers. The milking parlour seemed to confuse them, with its narrow, wet places to walk and heavy aromas of milk and manure. They probed among round hay bales and looked in the hay chopper. They contemplated inspecting the feeding face of the open pit silo but were concerned about the mess and the electric fence. One glance at Ferdinand was enough to discourage any further inspection there.

After an hour and a half, they thanked Rick for his cooperation and departed.

The team that visited Marie had much to look through in her shop and ended up in her kitchen, drinking coffee and discussing electric cars. The team that visited Mel had never seen a blacksmith shop before, except in books when they were kids. The hand-forged bear trap they found on the back wall was an object of intense amazement.

Mel's name was on a list of people with forest cabins in the region and the officers asked him if he could take them to his. Mel said he certainly could, but that there was no road and that the lakes were frozen, but not enough to support an ATV or a helicopter.

"You can get there with an hour or two of hard walking," he said, "if you bring along a good GPS unit."

As they talked, inspecting his cabin seemed to become less important. The officers were intrigued by the collections of empty rifle shells Mel had standing in rows on his shop windowsills. There were all kinds, including a few .30-30s, but these did not seem to stand out in importance for the officers.

The next day was Friday, blacksmith day for Rick and Mel. From the farm shop, Rick dug out a 10-foot length of carpet left over from some project of Uncle Gilles'. It was filthy now but conveniently wrapped around a hollow tube of thick cardboard.

Rick backed his truck up near Ferdinand's corral and found some old burlap bags in the feed room. He wrapped the rifle in the burlap and stuffed it into the carpet tube. Bronwyn already was loaded and ready to go, along with a collection of her favourite toys and distractions. The moment had come.

Rick hopped into the truck, pressed Bronwyn's nose like a button to make her laugh and drove off.

It was legal deer-hunting season now, and the Mounties who wanted to see all the .30-30s in the area were using this to their advantage. At the bottom of the west hill, they could stop most of the vehicles that were passing through the village and they were doing just that, pulling hunters over for a look at their guns. Rick rolled down his window as he stopped at the checkpoint.

"Are you going hunting at all today?" the officer asked. As she spoke, she looked in and saw Bronwyn in her car seat, looking back at her with bright-eyed interest. "Oh, maybe not, eh!" she said. "Can I just peek behind your seat, sir?"

Rick hopped out and pulled his seat forward so she could have a good look.

"What do you have in the back?" she asked.

"Some carpeting I'm giving away."

She strolled back and hefted the carpet roll with one hand. "Thanks for your cooperation."

She put a small yellow sticker on the back of his side-view mirror, which Rick supposed would signal that he already had been interviewed if he drove past the checkpoint again that day.

To be suitably nonchalant, he stopped at the café not far from the checkpoint and got two cups to go before heading over to Mel's place.

Mel already had the forge up to full heat and a playpen for Bronwyn set up on the shop floor, a safe distance away. Rick brought in the coffee, then the carpet and then Bronwyn.

They wasted no time. Mel hurriedly unpacked the rifle, removed the bolt, dismantled the trigger mechanism, and laid all the pieces at the side of the fire. The wooden rifle stock burned away in fifteen minutes in the hot forge, as Mel stirred the fire and Rick cranked the blower.

Mel told Rick what to do, task by task, and they worked like demons. They heated sections of the rifle barrel to an almost white heat and then hammered each onto a chisel to cut it off. They heated and hammered the bolt into an unrecognizable object and then heated and hammered flat each of the sections of the rifle barrel, obliterating the chamber and the inner barrel surfaces completely. The trigger and other metal bits became odd-shaped rods of steel.

Rick and Mel were working so intently that they did not notice that Constable Roger Laliberty had come into the shop at some point and was standing there now, watching them. He was in full duty uniform, bristling with equipment and a bullet-proof vest, and wore his uniform jacket against the cold outside.

They stopped abruptly. "Well, Roger!" Mel said somewhat uneasily, trying to contain his surprise and consternation. "You got an interest in blacksmith work?"

Roger walked in closer to the forge and anvil. "I've always wanted to try it," he said. "Do you ever give lessons?"

There was a pause and Roger stepped closer still. He picked up some tongs and used them to hold up one of the hot pieces of flattened gun barrel. "This is pretty good steel, isn't it?" he asked. "I've heard it's good for knife blades. Maybe you could teach me, and I could make a crooked knife from a bit of this stuff. I've always wanted one."

Neither Rick nor Mel had ever heard Roger sound so cagey. What was he up to? Did he really know what they were doing? It seemed that he was playing with them like a cat plays with a mouse it soon will chew up and swallow. But human cats are gloating when they play with their doomed mice, enjoying an ecstasy of power, and it was not at all Roger's way to flaunt his authority.

Roger walked over to a window and looked at the collection of empty brass rifle shells on the sill. He picked up several, looked at the bottom of each, chose one and turned back to Mel. "Purley Jordan told me the other day that you know how to make nice little brass rings out of old rifle shells. Is that true?"

"Why, yes, it is, Roger," Mel said with genuine surprise. "I used to make rings for the kids who would come visit the shop, years ago. There might still be a few around the village."

Roger handed the shell he had selected to Mel. "Can you show me how you do it?"

The shell was one of Mel's own .30-30 shells. Mel knew this because the firing pin in his old rifle had gotten badly out of alignment and hit the centrefire cap way out on its edge. "Sure. It only takes a few minutes to do."

He searched around on a shelf and came back with a kind of a tapered metal rod on a stand that fit into one of the holes on his anvil to hold it in place. He put the shell in a vice and knocked the cap out of it with a hammer and a long nail, creating a small hole where the cap had been.

Mel alternately heated the shell and hammered it gently with a jig down the tapered rod, bottom end first. The shell crumpled and then rolled and slid, half-melted, down the rod until it had become a shiny brass ring with no evidence that it had ever been a rifle shell.

"How old is your daughter?" Mel asked Roger.

"Fifteen."

Mel made the ring a little bigger by forcing it further down the tapered rod. He tapped it free, cooled it in water, and handed it to Roger. "Young girls these days seem to like thumb rings," he said.

Roger inspected the ring, tried it on his fingers until he found one that it loosely fit, and left it there. He reached into his jacket pocket and pulled out another empty rifle shell with a thick grey-green patina of age covering its external surface, and handed it to Mel. "Can you make a ring out of this one, too?"

Mel inspected the shell. It was a .30-30. The dent from the firing pin on the centrefire cap was way off to one side. Rick, standing behind Mel, could see that, too.

"I picked this up a while ago," Roger said.

Mel looked at the shell and looked at Roger.

"When Purley told me that you could make brass rings from shells, I thought maybe you would make this one into a ring for me."

Mel surged into action. He knocked out the cap and gently heated the shell. Rick picked Bronwyn out of the play pen, where she was acting bored, and they all watched as the old .30-30 shell lost all trace of its original purpose and became a shiny brass ring.

"What size for this one?" Mel asked.

"I want it for my son," Roger said. "He just started law school. He is going to be wrestling with justice for the rest of his life. There are some kinds of justice that the law of the land and its agents, like me, struggle hard to achieve. They are raw, and dangerous, and often go wrong. But the law of the land also can go wrong. There is a rare balance of justice in that ring you've just made. I want him to keep that balance close to him."

Mel turned back to the ring, lightly heating it once again and tapping it to a wider diameter. He knocked it loose, removed and cooled it and took it to a side counter where he rummaged in a drawer. He pulled out a little jewellery-store box from which he removed an elegant gold necklace chain.

"I tried making jewellery once," he said. "I was never any good at it, but your son might like his ring this way."

He unclasped the chain, threaded it through the brass ring, and clasped it again. He held up the chain and ring to look it over and seemed satisfied. Then he put them in the box and handed it to Roger. "Maybe he can hang that up on his law degree."

Roger nodded his gratitude. He put the little box deep into his jacket pocket. "I have to go, now. I'm due for a shift at the rifle check station."

He stopped beside Rick and took the first brass ring off his finger to show Bronwyn. "I'd give this to you, but you'd swallow it," he told her, which was certainly true.

He waved and was gone.

Mel and Rick stood still and stared at each other for half an eternity.

Finally, Mel broke the spell. "There's good people in this world, Rick. Let's not forget that."

They cleaned up and checked to make sure that they had completed every aspect of their job.

Mel said that, despite the cold, he needed a break and was going to go dig himself a mess of clams that afternoon. He knew a good spot that was still open, and he was going to take Jerry along to see how he might take to clamming. If all they did was play with crabs and look at sand worms, that would be just fine.

He picked up his clam hack and bucket, and the three conspirators walked out of the shop together. As he got into his truck, Rick noticed a yellow sticker on the back of Mel's side-view mirror on the driver's side—a free pass from Roger.

Bronwyn was tired and hungry, and so was Rick. It was a short drive back to the farm. Warm milk for

Bronwyn, warm chili for Rick, clean-up, load of laundry in the washer, diaper change, and nap time. Bronwyn was almost asleep already.

Rick was supposed to be at the weekly dairy management meeting in half an hour. He weighed his priorities. He carried Bronwyn into his and Zora's bedroom, made a nest for himself and Bronnie in the middle of the big bed and turned off his phone.

Cuddled together, they drifted off to sleep.

Ted Leighton

Acknowledgements

Some components in this novel were inspired by stories told within my family and particularly by my father, Alexander Leighton (1908 – 2007), who was a child and young man in Digby County from 1914 to 1930 and returned to work there in 1948.

The expert editing of Andrew Wetmore of Moose House Publications, as well as his encouragement and gracious good humour, improved the manuscript in innumerable ways and assured its completion.

I am deeply grateful to Moose House Publications for recognizing sufficient merit in the work to undertake its publication, and to several personal friends who read previous drafts and urged me on to continue.

In Chapter 17, Rick's old colleague, Wade, refers to Wade Davis's 1985 book, *The Serpent and the Rainbow: a Harvard scientist's astonishing journey into the secret societies of Haitian voodoo, zombis, and magic*. It was published by Simon & Schuster, and is still available in print and e-book editions.

About the author

Ted Leighton (O.C.) lives and writes in Digby and Annapolis Counties in Western Nova Scotia, where he spent his formative childhood and to which he returned in 2015. In addition to fiction, he has published non-fiction as a teacher and scientist at the Western College of Veterinary Medicine, where he remains professor emeritus.

He is a *professeur associé* (adjunct professor) at Université Sainte-Anne, the conservation guardian of Bear Island in the Annapolis Basin, and a promoter of traditional Celtic music, which he plays on the uilleann pipes.

This is his first novel.

CPSIA information can be obtained
at www.ICGtesting.com
Printed in the USA
BVHW030437231022
650037BV00007B/140

9 781990 187445